The sudden darkness blinded her and whispered of secrets and of something terribly wrong. Now she wanted only to escape the room and the rows of books that offered innocent faces to hide what lay behind. But she took no more than three steps toward the door before her way was blocked.

A shadow loomed against the light as a figure stood in the opening. Recognition was not possible in so brief a glimpse. The person stepped into the room and closed the door very softly behind. She was shut into utter blackness with someone who moved with stealth and who knew his way across the room without hesitation. . . .

BOOKS BY PHYLLIS A. WHITNEY

THE SINGING STONES*
RAINBOW IN THE MIST*
FEATHER ON THE MOON*
SILVERSWORD*
FLAMING TREE*
DREAM OF ORCHIDS*
RAINSONG*
EMERALD*
VERMILION*
POINCIANA*
DOMINO*
THE GLASS FLAME*
THE STONE BULL*
THE GOLDEN UNICORN*
SPINDRIFT*
THE TURQUOISE MASK*
SNOWFIRE*
LISTEN FOR THE
   WHISPERER*
LOST ISLAND*
THE WINTER PEOPLE*
HUNTER'S GREEN*
SILVERHILL*
COLUMBELLA*
SEA JADE*
BLACK AMBER*
SEVEN TEARS FOR
   APOLLO*
WINDOW ON THE
   SQUARE*

BLUE FIRE*
THUNDER HEIGHTS*
THE MOONFLOWER*
SKYE CAMERON*
THE TREMBLING HILLS*
THE QUICKSILVER POOL*
THE RED CARNELIAN

Young Adult Novels
STEP TO THE MUSIC*
THE FIRE AND
   THE GOLD*
MYSTERY OF THE BLACK
   DIAMONDS
NOBODY LIKES TRINA
SECRET OF THE STONE
   FACE
MYSTERY OF THE
   GOLDEN HORN*
MYSTERY ON THE ISLE OF
   SKYE*

Adult Nonfiction
A GUIDE TO FICTION
   WRITING
WRITING JUVENILE
   STORIES AND NOVELS

*Published by Fawcett Books

MYSTERY OF THE HIDDEN HAND

Phyllis A. Whitney

FAWCETT JUNIPER • NEW YORK

RLI: $\dfrac{\text{VL 6 \& up}}{\text{IL 7 \& up}}$

A Fawcett Juniper Book
Published by Ballantine Books
Copyright © 1963 by Phyllis A. Whitney
Copyright renewed 1991 by Phyllis A. Whitney

Library of Congress Catalog Card Number: 63-11840

ISBN 0-449-70365-7

Manufactured in the United States of America

First Ballantine Books Edition: November 1991

For Barbara, Michael, and Lorraine
With love,
From Grandmother Phyllis

Contents

1

*The Figure
in the Cape*

It was a Saturday morning in early June on the Greek island of Rhodes. In a bedroom on the fourth and top floor of the Hotel Hermes an American girl, Gale Tyler, was getting dressed for her first morning on the island. In the adjoining room her brother Warren was already up and ready for the day. Neither Gale nor Warren had any idea of the strange events that had just begun on the lower floor—events that would soon involve them in unexpected adventure.

At that very moment, on the lobby floor of the hotel, a door opened quietly and an eerie figure stepped through it. The figure was hidden from head to foot by a voluminous black cape, topped by a black hood that engulfed the head of the wearer. No one noticed this odd spectacle because the hotel guests were breakfasting in a dining room off the far end of the lobby. The clerk at the desk was studying his register book and did not look up.

The black-clothed figure ran softly toward the stairs that led to the second floor and flew up them. "Flew" is the right word, for the cape soared like wings and the swift movement was like the darting of a bat. It passed the second-floor landing and mounted to the third. There it halted at the end of the long, uncarpeted corridor, pausing as if to listen.

No door on the corridor opened. Nothing stirred for its entire length. The figure took flight again, running down the hall with long, leaping strides that resulted in great speed and a number of thuds along the way wherever it lighted.

Behind the row of third-floor doors a late sleeper was awakened by one of those thuds. She turned over in bed and looked about her crossly. She was a small woman, rather young, with short black hair tousled from sleeping. Had she smiled, she might have been pretty. The scowl with which she greeted the morning did not become her, but she would never see it, because when she looked into her mirror she always put on her best face.

The young woman's dream had not been pleasant, and neither was her awakening. With no notion of the black figure darting past her door, she considered her various misfortunes and humiliations, while the scowl deepened and dark thoughts began to stir once more in her mind.

This was her first morning back in Rhodes since she had left the island for America six years before. She had not thought of paying off an old score, had not thought of getting even at that time. Feeling humiliated and angry, as well as desolate over her sister's death, she had gone to America. There she had met and married a Greek-American. Now he was dead, and she had come home to Greece. Here in Rhodes, old memories had begun to stir. When she discovered who it was who owned this new hotel, she had taken the first step and moved in as a guest. She knew she looked very different now than when she had left. Much more stylish, she thought with satisfaction. So far, no one had recognized her.

She had no idea how she would execute her purpose, but she had every intention of punishing the one who had humiliated and injured her. As she lay in bed she allowed her thoughts to smolder. Holding up one hand, she turned it this way and that, as if it would give her some answer to a puzzle. She did not know as yet the meaning of that other hand she had seen long ago in Rhodes—a hand with the fingers outstretched as if in pleading. But she knew it meant something that would be useful to her now. She must seek the answer if she was to be revenged upon her enemy.

Outside in the corridor, the black-winged figure had reached the stairs at the far end and started up them to the fourth floor, the cape still billowing behind. This time there was no pause for listening. Away went the figure, leaping and running the full length of the fourth-floor hall. With its back turned, it did not see the boy who opened his door a slit to look out in astonishment as the flying black figure went by.

When it whirled at the end to retrace its steps, Warren Tyler closed his own door hastily and crossed the bedroom to his sister's door.

"Gale!" he called softly. "Hey, Gale—are you up?"

In the next room his sister was dressed except for her shoes. At his urgent call, she ran in her socks to the door between their rooms and pulled it open.

"What's the matter?"

"Something funny's going on," Warren said. "Come here and have a look."

She joined him, and they peered together through the slit. The figure did not look around. It whirled with a great rustle of silk and went off down the hall with those great leaps. But this time it came to a sudden halt halfway to the end and paused beside a closed door. A hand darted from among the folds, turned the knob, and with a swoop of flying black cloth the entire apparition disappeared into the room and shut the door behind it.

Gale and Warren stared at each other. Both were brown-haired, and there was a marked brother-and-sister resemblance between them. Warren was a slender, wiry boy of thirteen, with dark eyes that had a tendency to go dreamy when he was off in a world of his own. Of the two he seemed the more serious. Gale was a year younger. Her eyes had an alert, interested look in them, and there were laugh quirks at the corners of her mouth.

"Where's Mother?" she whispered. "Does she know about this?"

"She's gone down to breakfast. She said to let you sleep. Come along and don't make any noise."

"Isn't this whole floor supposed to be empty?" she whispered, tiptoeing after Warren in her socks.

"That's what Aunt Marjorie said," Warren agreed.

"Since the hotel has just opened, she said they didn't expect to fill it the first season and we could have this floor to ourselves."

Aunt Marjorie, Mother's sister, was the American wife of Alexandros Castelis of Rhodes. Her husband had recently bought this hotel, and they were running it for the first year. Since Mr. Tyler had been sent on a United States Government mission to Athens, this had been a wonderful opportunity for Mother to visit her sister Marjorie in Rhodes. Dad had been left in Athens yesterday, and the others had arrived by plane last night. Gale had been looking forward to meeting their cousin Anastasia, but Aunt Marjorie had said that she had a previous engagement and so could not be there to greet them. Now Gale was hoping to see her at breakfast.

Outside the closed door the two paused to listen. Some very curious noises were issuing from beyond it. It sounded to Gale as though someone were climbing onto a table or a high bureau and then jumping off. There were thuds and bumps and grunts. And once a groan, as if of pain.

While the two listened in bewilderment, a fourth person appeared from the stairs at the far end and came toward them. She was a small woman, hardly taller than Warren, dressed in pajamas and a green robe. Her short black hair had obviously not seen a comb since she got out of bed, and she was popping mad. She gave the two near the door a scowl that seemed to dismiss them as persons of no importance. All her attention was for the door, through which could be heard the effect of someone jumping heavily off the top of a bureau.

The angry young woman pounded on the door. At once there was silence beyond—silence followed by a soft sound like the rustling of silk. Then silence again. When there was no answer to her knock, the woman turned the doorknob and pushed her way into the room.

Looking over Warren's shoulder, Gale saw to her surprise that the space within was empty. No black-cloaked figure was in view, and there was not even a chair from which anyone could have jumped; in fact, there was not a stick of furniture of any kind in the entire room. Only shuttered doors, opening on the long balcony that fronted the hotel, revealed a way of escape.

The little woman pulled open a closet door to look angrily inside. She kicked at a cardboard carton within and slammed the door shut. Then she went out on the balcony.

Gale and Warren had remained just outside the door, and as the woman stepped onto the balcony, they saw another door open at one end of the corridor. The figure in cloak and hood darted out and flew in a billow of black wings toward the stairs, moving now with hardly a sound as it disappeared down them.

The angry young woman returned from the balcony and rejoined the two in the corridor. As she neared them, Gale noticed the strong perfume with which she must have drenched her robe—a spicy, pungent scent like that of geraniums. Now her attention focused on the two young people for the first time.

"So!" she cried. "It was you jumping about in that room right over my head! Waking me out of a sound sleep. Disturbing me when I am very tired and need my rest!''

She spoke English like someone who had learned the language in America, and she spoke it with an accent—probably Greek, Gale thought. What she said was silly, since she had stood outside the door beside them and had heard the jarring thuds inside the room. It was probable that she was so angry that anyone at all would do as an outlet for her rage.

Warren said calmly: ''It wasn't us. We haven't been in that room at all. The one you're looking for—''

Gale nudged him with her elbow. She did not like the manner of this cross little woman. For some reason she put herself on the side of the queerly behaving person in the black cape.

''We don't know who it was,'' she said quickly, and Warren did not contradict her. It was perfectly true that they had no idea who the figure in the cape might be.

The little woman swung away from them for another look about the room. This time Warren stepped inside to look too, and Gale followed him. At that moment a small, dazzling circle of light flashed through the balcony doors and caught the small woman in the eye, momentarily blinding her. She clapped her hands to her face to shut out the dazzle, and the patch of light sped on around the walls of the room.

''It's nothing,'' Warren said. ''Probably the sun caught a side mirror on a car as it turned a corner.''

But it was clear almost at once that he was wrong. The dazzle of light remained, and it took on a sort of pulse. It was as if someone put a hand over the source, intercepting the reflection, only to block it out again.

"Someone is signaling," the woman said sharply. "Signaling to a person who waited in this room."

She edged toward the balcony and looked into the distance from which the signals seemed to be coming. Then she glanced over her shoulder at Warren.

"Come here, boy," she said rudely. "Come here and tell me from what house the signals come."

Warren went out on the balcony to seek the source, and again Gale followed. It was easy enough to pick out the house from which the mirror continued to signal. It was a big white house two or three blocks away, two stories high, and set in the midst of a lush, green area of trees and garden. From one of the upper windows the mirror flash came once more—then ceased for good.

The small woman had stopped scowling, and Gale saw that she was rather pretty when she didn't look so sullen. She appeared suddenly pleased and interested, almost like a person with a secret.

"Yes," she said softly, "that is the house. The house of my enemy."

Then, without another word, she turned and walked from the room, leaving Gale and Warren to stare at each other in astonishment.

"Maybe you'd better pinch me to see if I'm awake," Gale said.

Warren grinned and reached out a ready hand. Gale ducked just in time.

"Can you figure any of this out?" she asked. "People who fly around in black capes and jump off furniture that isn't there! Mirror signals! And a lady soaked in geraniums who talks about an enemy.''

Warren shook his head. ''I suppose it all has a simple enough answer if we just had the key.''

They stepped out on the quiet balcony again. Below them a line of palm trees threw early-morning shadows across the pavement. A few blocks away the blue Aegean lay shining in the sun, the soft rushing sound of its waves on the island shore reaching them clearly. Across the water rose the high, blue mountains of Turkey. The white house stood peacefully among its trees. No one stirred in the residential street below the balcony. There was a scent of flowers on the air. Yet when they turned back to the room and went through it, Gale could smell only the sharp, disturbing odor of geraniums.

''Something is certainly going on in this hotel,'' she said to her brother. ''Something awfully queer.''

He nodded. ''Maybe we'd better tell Aunt Marjorie. Get your shoes on and we'll go down to breakfast.''

She started for her room and then hesitated. ''Let's not say anything right away. We can't tell whom we might get into trouble. I don't think I like that woman very much, but we don't know who the other person is.''

Warren agreed and closed the door upon the empty room. ''I'm going down for breakfast,'' he said.

Gale ran to put on her shoes, suddenly aware of how hungry she was.

❦ ❦

2

The Scarlet Crab

By the time they reached the hotel dining room, bright with the morning sun streaming through its windows, most of the guests had finished breakfast and the room was emptying. Mrs. Tyler sat alone at a table, with a cup of coffee beside her plate, and she looked around, smiling as they came in.

Gale found herself approving once more of her mother's appearance. Her curly brown hair was brushed neatly back from her forehead. Her blue dress looked as though it had just been pressed, though it must have been taken from a suitcase last night. Her brown eyes were interested, eager, and friendly. People often said that Gale's eyes were like her mother's.

"Hi, sleepyheads," Mother said. "Come along and order. I'll sit with you while you eat."

"Has Anastasia come down yet?" Gale asked as she and Warren slipped into their places.

"I still haven't met her," Mother said. "She was up early for breakfast with her mother and father and then went out on an errand. Isn't this a pleasant hotel? Sort of small and neighborly."

A friendly young Greek boy, who spoke only a little English, waited on their table. Gale ate in silence and let her mother and Warren do the talking. She was thinking again of her cousin Anastasia, whom she had yet to meet. There was something she had in common with Anastasia that might help to make them good friends. Both girls had older sisters. Not ordinary older sisters, but ones that were altogether special.

Gale sighed comfortably and spread the delicious Greek honey on her toast. The comfortable feeling came from the fact that Audrey had other plans for this time of year and had not come with them on the trip. It was nice to be in a place where no one knew Audrey. There would be no one to say, "So you're Audrey Tyler's younger sister—" and then start measuring Gale against Audrey in a way that was sure to find Gale wanting. How could they help it when Audrey was so pretty and clever? She always got wonderful marks in school, and she could paint and sing and write and dance, while Gale could do none of these things. She loved and admired her sister, but she didn't want to compete with her all the time.

Not so long ago Gale and her father had talked over the problem of Audrey, and after that she had felt better about the whole thing. Dad had made her understand that neither he nor Mother expected two Audrey's in the same family. They wanted Gale to be her own independent self, and undoubtedly one of these days she would discover some talents and interests of her own. She was still young—there was plenty of time.

Gale had wondered how Anastasia felt about being the younger sister of a famous ballet dancer like Lexine Casteli. Did Anastasia endure the same problem of having people expect her to live up to her sister? It would be interesting to find out. Gale was looking forward to meeting her half-Greek, half-American cousin.

Mother looked around toward the door, and Gale saw Aunt Marjorie coming across the dining room. She looked a little like Mother, except that she was smaller. As sisters, their interests had always been somewhat alike, but without any special talents to make one of them stand out. The sister problem had not been the same with them.

Marjorie Casteli stopped beside their table with a smiling "Good morning." There was an odd custom, Gale had learned, about Greek last names. The name by which the wife was called often took a different ending from her husband's. Thus Alexandros Castelis' wife became Mrs. Casteli.

"I'm off to market this morning," Aunt Marjorie told her sister. "Would you like to come along? That is, if Warren and Gale don't mind losing you for an hour or so. This afternoon Anastasia plans to take you all on a visit to the old City of the Knights. I hope you'll enjoy that."

Warren looked interested at once. His absorption in ancient things dated back several years. At first Dad had thought he was going through the "buried treasure" phase, but his interest had lasted and War-

ren had continued to be fascinated by archaeology.
Coming to Greece had been an enormously exciting
thing for him. Yesterday, during their several hours'
wait in Athens between planes, it had been hard to
drag Warren away from the museums and the Acropolis.

"I'd love to go marketing with you," Mother said
to Aunt Marjorie. "I'm sure Warren and Gale can
amuse themselves around the hotel this morning. Let
me finish my coffee and I'll be ready."

Aunt Marjorie stood beside their table, talking
while she waited. "This morning I had a long distance call from Lexine in London. Wonderful news!
She's to dance the role of Helen in a special ballet
performance of *Helen of Troy* in the ancient theater
in Delphi next month. But she's coming to Rhodes
for a visit first. Perhaps in another week or two."

That meant Anastasia would have her gifted sister
right here in Rhodes, Gale thought, and wondered
how her cousin would feel about that.

"How very exciting," Mother said warmly. "It will
be especially nice for us to meet Lexine."

Aunt Marjorie was plainly elated about her famous
daughter's coming. "Imagine me—the mother of a
prima ballerina! Sometimes I can hardly believe it
myself."

"I know how you feel," said Mother. "While Audrey is younger and hasn't launched herself in any
one direction yet, she's gifted in so many ways that
sometimes she overwhelms me."

Her sister smiled and reached out to pat Gale's
hand. "Never mind! My Anastasia and your Gale will
hold us both down to earth."

Gale understood that the remark was meant in a humorous way, but she winced in spite of herself. Even though her father and mother did not expect her to be another Audrey, it would have been nice to have some sort of special gift all her own. Had Anastasia one? she wondered.

Her thoughts were interrupted because at that moment a strangely exotic-looking woman walked into the dining room. She ignored the waiter who tried to lead her to a table, and came directly to where Aunt Marjorie stood.

For just a moment Gale did not recognize her as the tousle-haired, scowling little woman of their recent encounter upstairs. The short black hair had vanished, and in its place was an amazing pile, the color of peanut butter, built on top of her head. Over each eye was a patch of bright blue, smudged clear to her very black eyebrows. The rest of her face was pale, and she wore no lipstick at all. Her dress was a bright green print, and her sandaled feet were bare. Again the scent of geraniums enveloped her, and Gale could not help a rather violent sneeze as she neared their table.

Aunt Marjorie turned toward her pleasantly. "Good morning, Mrs. Lambrou. I hope you slept well last night."

The blue-smeared eyes were angry and hostile; the pale, tight lips did not smile.

"I would have slept better," the woman said, "if there had not been some creature leaping and jumping all about the room directly over my head ever since dawn this morning."

The lady was not altogether truthful, Gale thought.

It had been much later than dawn that she must have been awakened. She did not seem to notice Warren and Gale there at the table, but went right on with her complaint.

At last Aunt Marjorie broke in. "I can't understand this. The room above you is empty. I can't imagine what could have made so much noise. If you like, we can move you to another room."

"I prefer to stay where I am," the woman said. "Provided this does not happen again." She nodded stiffly to Aunt Marjorie and went off to her table—a top-heavy little figure beneath the mountain of peanut-butter hair.

Warren whistled softly under his breath. "How did she manage that? When we saw her upstairs her hair was black."

"It's a wig," Gale whispered. She had occasionally seen women in Washington and New York wearing such concoctions on their heads and had thought them rather funny. But Mrs. Lambrou's hairdo was the most astonishing creation she had ever seen.

"Who is that?" Mother asked, trying not to smile.

Aunt Marjorie raised her eyebrows in an expressive manner. "Her name is Geneva Lambrou. I understand she was born in Lindos, here in Rhodes. She tells me she went to America about six years ago and married there. Now she is a widow, and she has come home. I hope she isn't going to be a difficult guest. I'll have to look into this matter of the jumping. I have a faint suspicion—" she smiled and broke off. "Are you through with your coffee, Bea? If you are, let's get started. The car is out in front."

When Mother and Aunt Marjorie had gone, Gale

waited impatiently for Warren to finish eating. The moment his last mouthful was down, she made her suggestion. "Let's go upstairs and have another look at that room. Maybe we can find out what's going on. Then we can see if it's something we ought to tell Aunt Marjorie."

Warren was willing, and they left the dining room together. They did not wait for the elevator, but hurried up the curving stairs to the fourth floor. On the lower floor maids were working in and out of the bedrooms, but they had not reached the top floor yet.

Gale remembered the room number, and they went to the right door and opened it cautiously. The room was empty, and they went inside. Warren looked out upon the balcony at once, but no one was there. Mother had said clothes closets were unusual in Europe, but since this was a new hotel, each room had one. The closet door was still ajar as Mrs. Lambrou had left it, and Gale saw the cardboard carton she had kicked. She pulled it into the room and knelt before it.

The top flaps were open, and it seemed to contain odds and ends of clothing. Idly she drew out a mass of soft black jersey. When she held it up she saw that it was a dancer's leotard. Warren had come to watch, and he reached in and lifted out a black cloth bundle.

"There's something here," he said, and unfolded it to reveal the pieces of a broken dish that had been wrapped in a pair of black tights. Warren set the broken wedges on the floor, and the three jagged pieces fitted together in a brightly colored pattern of small green ships with white sails, afloat against a rusty-red background. But what an odd place to put a broken dish!

Gale had an uneasy feeling that they should not be poking into someone else's possessions like this, but the carton was as fascinating as a grab bag. She reached in and pulled out a pair of worn pink ballet slippers and then a second leotard wrapped about something hard and crunchy.

"These things must belong to Lexine," she said. "They're all for dancing. Maybe we shouldn't take out anything more."

Warren began to wrap up the broken plate. "Anyway, old clothes won't tell us what has been happening in this room."

Gale put the slippers back and then unfolded the leotard. Wrapped into it, in a torn scrap of Greek newspaper, were bits of something hard like stone. Before she could examine her find more closely, the hall door banged open without warning, and the familiar figure in black cape and hood blew into the room as if on the wings of a storm.

Gale stared in astonishment, the wadded packet half hidden in one hand, the leotard dangling from the other. Warren looked up from putting the bundle of tights and broken plate in the carton, startled but unfrightened.

Thanks to the huge, drooping hood that hung over the figure's face, leaving it in dark shadow, nothing could be seen of the hidden person except a pair of small, angry hands. They jerked the carton out of Warren's grasp and began to shove it into the closet, while their owner chattered angrily in Greek. Hidden eyes beneath the hood noted the leotard in Gale's limp hand and snatched it away to thrust into the box. The carton was shoved through the closet door and kicked into place. A little indignantly, Gale put the paper-wrapped packet behind her back.

Warren recovered first. He slipped around behind the figure as it struggled with the carton. Just as it straightened up, he tweaked off the hood. It fell back from curly black hair, and the figure whirled to face them. Gale found herself looking into the pretty, indignant face of a girl about her own age. It was a face she had seen in snapshots Aunt Marjorie had sent home from Greece. This, quite evidently, was Anastasia.

Now that she stood revealed, the girl stopped speaking in Greek.

"Why do you come into this room and search in other people's things?" she demanded angrily. "It is no business of yours what is put into a box in this room!"

Gale felt only dismay and regret. This seemed a bad beginning for a friendship she had looked forward to.

"You're Anastasia, aren't you?" she asked, sounding as apologetic as she could.

Bright color bloomed in the girl's face, and her dark eyes sparkled as if with tears—which seemed a very strange thing. She managed to control herself with an effort.

"I am Tassoula," she said. "Why did you come to this room? Do they teach you no manners in America?"

In spite of her words, Gale had a feeling that this girl was oddly frightened about something. She wanted to reach out to touch and quiet her, to tell her that whatever it was she wanted to hide, no one would betray her secret. But Warren gave her no chance to speak.

"So it was you jumping around in the room this morning, disturbing Mrs. Lambrou?" he said calmly.

"I was not jumping!" said Tassoula.

"We didn't tell Mrs. Lambrou—" Gale began, but Warren went right on.

"Maybe those mirror signals were for you?" he speculated.

The girl stared at him. "Mirror signals? In this room?"

He nodded. "Somebody over in that big white house two or three blocks away was sending mirror flashes into this room."

All the anger went out of the girl's flushed face, to be replaced by a look of eagerness and excitement. Without another word, she ran to the door and flew off down the hall in her ballooning black cape. Only her curly dark hair was uncovered, and she did not bother now to pull up the hood.

"I hope she doesn't run smack into Mrs. Lambrou," Warren said. "What do you suppose that was all about?"

Gale could only shake her head. If this had really been their first introduction to their cousin Anastasia, it was certainly a disappointment. But why had the girl said her name was Tassoula? She certainly looked like the girl in those snapshots.

With one foot, Warren gave the carton a final shove into the closet and closed the door on it. The mystery, whatever it was, had not progressed very far toward a solution. The only thing they knew at the moment was that the figure in the black cape was a young girl of Gale's age. From her appearance she might be Greek or American, or a mixture of both. While she spoke English well and with an American pronunciation to the words, there was a slight accent, a "tune" of inflection that was different.

Warren turned toward the door, and Gale followed him from the room. "I used up my film in Athens yesterday," he said. "I'm going to load my camera."

Gale welcomed a chance to be alone. She returned to her room and sat on the bed, looking about with satisfaction. It was a pleasant room, bright and plain, with white walls and ceiling and simple modern furniture. On one wall hung a framed photograph of Grecian columns looking lonely and very beautiful on the edge of a steep cliff. But it was the paper-wrapped packet that interested her most of all now.

Carefully she opened her fingers and examined the strange contents. Again this was something that had been broken into bits—much smaller bits, however, than the large wedges of plate. Poking among the pieces, she found that they were glazed and painted on one side. The other side of each piece was the unglazed color of baked clay. She picked out a blue bit that looked like the tail of a fish, and here was the craggy, red claw of a crab. Putting the pieces together was like working a jigsaw puzzle, and she persisted until all the broken sections were in place and she could regard the result in mystified wonder.

The whole seemed to be a ceramic tile about five inches square. On it had been painted a portion of an underwater scene. There was a pale sea-green background in which swam a tiny blue fish and a scarlet crab. Bits of swaying yellow seaweed and red coral further indicated depths of the sea. Part of the crab's right claw was missing, as if the picture might continue onto another tile.

The whole had been smashed beyond repair and was ready only to be thrown away. How very strange that it should have been so carefully wrapped in paper and tucked into the folds of a leotard! Perhaps, as Warren said, all this made sense when one had the key, but Gale had no key at all, and the longer she looked at the tile and considered the behavior of the girl in the black cape, the greater her bewilderment grew. What had those mirror signals meant that they had so excited Tassoula and sent her running from the room? Who lived in that big white house?

At last she gathered up the bits and put them all in an ashtray on her bed table. She couldn't solve the problem by staring at the pieces.

Warren looked through the connecting door. "I think I'll go for a walk and take some pictures," he said. "Want to come along?"

Gale jumped up to join him at once. He slung his camera strap over his shoulder, and they went downstairs together. On the way they met neither Mrs. Lambrou nor the girl in the black cape.

At the desk Uncle Alexandros looked up and smiled at them. He was a large, handsome man with bright, dark eyes. Last night when he had driven them home from the airport, he had talked a great deal in a cheerful, friendly manner. He had sounded hospitable and happy to have them here, but Gale still felt a little strange and uncertain with him. He nodded his approval of their going out, and they crossed the lobby. In a niche near the door was a statue, a small copy, Uncle Alexandros had said, of the famous statue of Hermes holding the baby Dionysus—the original of which was preserved in the museum of Olympia.

Outdoors the bright, clear air of Rhodes had a sparkle to it, and there was a salty tang you could almost taste on your lips. The wind from the sea was cool and bracing.

"Let's go over to the water," Warren said.

On the way downstairs a plan had come into Gale's mind, and she shook her head. It was something she wanted to try by herself.

"I think I'll walk down one of these little streets and look at the gardens," she told him. "You go ahead. You'll be taking pictures anyway."

Warren didn't mind. When he was fiddling with camera stops and settings, everyone else had to wait. He didn't like to be hurried; so he wouldn't mind walking around alone.

He turned toward the water, and Gale took the opposite direction. Not far away a big white house in a garden was waiting for her. A house from whose upper windows had come the flashing of a mirror. While the house was no longer visible from the ground, she felt sure she could find it. It might be interesting to walk past its gate and see what sort of people lived there.

3

A Secret Message

The street took pleasant turns, and she chose the right-hand one and walked past a garden wall where bougainvillea grew in great purple-pink masses. She could see the tops of palm trees and the lance-shaped leaves of tall oleander bushes, abloom with clusters of red blossoms. The air had the heavenly scent of many flowers, and when a Greek boy came out of a nearby garden she saw that he wore a red hibiscus bloom tucked casually behind one ear.

She had chosen correctly, and through an opening in the trees she glimpsed the flat square roof of the white house. The trees and a high stone wall hid the structure, and she could get nothing more than a brief glimpse above the wall. Very slowly she walked past the place where a driveway ran between the stone pillars of a gate. To her disappointment, the drive turned and vanished amid plane trees, so she still could not see the house. The second time she passed the open gate, she came a little closer. There was a name plate on one stone pillar, but of course it was in Greek and she could not read the name of the owner.

The open gateway invited her, the driveway beckoned, the oleanders nodded their welcome in a breeze that blew briskly from the sea. Surely it would do no harm to accept the invitation just for a moment. She walked through the gate and a little way up the drive. Trees still hid the house in a most tantalizing way. Spreading out beside the drive was a stretch of green lawn, its grassy expanse narrowing to wind its way around a thicket of rhododendrons. Throwing caution aside, Gale left the drive and ran lightly across the lawn and around the huge clump of bushes.

Now the house was in full view, and she stood quite still to stare in admiration. The structure shone a dazzling white in the sun, and though it was square and without cupola or tower, it was beautifully clean of line. Across the face of the upper story ran a balcony with an intricate wrought-iron rail and arched spaces between slim columns.

No one appeared, either upstairs or down. It was quiet, except for the singing of birds in the trees and the rushing sounds of wind and sea that Gale was beginning to recognize as a familiar part of Rhodes. She had no notion that anyone was nearby and sprang about startled when something touched her from behind.

In dismay she found herself facing an old man who sat on a marble bench, half hidden by the rhododendron bushes. His thick hair was almost white, but his fierce eyebrows were still dark. Beneath them dark eyes watched her in a not unfriendly fashion. She had turned in time to see him pull back a knobby brown cane, and knew that he must have tapped her with it.

"Good morning," the old man said in English. "I see that you are admiring my house."

She was relieved that he was not angry over her trespassing. "It—it's a very interesting house," she offered hesitantly.

"The architecture is rather a mixture," he said amiably. "Turkish on Greek, you might say. It was built by the Turks many years ago when they occupied our island. Now that you are here, perhaps you would like to see a little more. I take it that you are an American visitor."

Gale nodded. "I'd like that. I could see the top of the house from our hotel this morning, and I walked over here to have a closer look."

"Ah?" said her host with interest. "Then you must be staying at the new hotel—the Hermes?"

Gale nodded. "Yes—my aunt and uncle own it. Mr. and Mrs. Alexandros Castelis. My name is Gale Tyler."

The old man seemed to find this information both interesting and gratifying. He stood up and made her a bow in an old-fashioned manner.

"In a sense we are related," he told her. "Permit me to introduce myself. I am Athanasios Castelis. Alexandros is my son."

Gale smiled at him in pleased surprise. "Then you must be Anastasia's grandfather?"

"That is so," he said. "Tassoula is indeed my granddaughter."

There was that puzzling name again. "Tassoula?" she repeated.

"That is what you might call a pet name for Anastasia. It means the little Anastasia. Our Greek names are so long and difficult that we shorten them to nicknames. For instance, my grandson Nicolas, Tassoula's cousin, is called Nicos. And I, with the longest name of all, am known to my friends as Thanos. But come, I must show you my house. My daughter-in-law Vera, Nicos' mother, is away at her shop in the old city; so I shall take you about myself."

As he rose from the marble bench, Gale noticed that the knobby end of his cane was carved in the form of an animal's head. He saw her interest and held it out for her to examine. The head, with its gaping mouth and strange, hollow eyes, was like no creature she had ever seen.

"It is a carving I made myself," the old man told her. "My inspiration was a stone lion in the Rhodes museum."

They walked through the garden together, the elderly Greek man and the young American girl. Oddly, there was an ease between them, as of two who recognized in each other a sympathetic spirit. Gale found that she was not shy with Tassoula's grandfather, as she was with busy Uncle Alexandros.

Before the steps of the house they came upon an open space patterned in small black and white pebbles set into a geometric design.

"Another Turkish touch," the old man said. "Did you know that the pebbles that make up the interior of the Children's Fountain at the United Nations are pebbles such as these, collected and sent by children from the island of Rhodes?''

Gale remembered having seen the fountain in New York, and she gazed at the stones with new interest.

A maid came to the door when the old man called, and he spoke a few words to her in Greek.

''I have ordered a typical Greek refreshment for you,'' he told Gale. ''It will be brought upstairs to my study.''

The house was airy and cool inside, with high ceilings and wide hallways. Her host took her hospitably from room to room downstairs, and she was aware of a great deal of dark woodwork, lustrous and shining with polish, of fine paintings on the walls, and art objects all around. The house reminded her a little of a museum, though she did not say so.

As she walked about, looking at everything, listening to her friendly guide, her mind was busy on other matters as well. It had been a great surprise to find that this house belonged to the Castelis family. But it explained things in a way. She wondered if it had been Anastasia's cousin, Nicos, who had been signalling the hotel with mirror flashes that morning to get his cousin's attention. It seemed likely, though rather odd. When they lived so close, and had telephones besides, why should such a manner of communication be necessary?

She had solved nothing of the puzzle by the time the old man started up a broad, turning flight of stairs and led the way to a second-floor room at the back of the house. The door stood open and he waved her in ahead of him.

Under Gale's feet the rug was a beautiful dark red,

with an all-over design in an oriental pattern. At the other end of the room was a big fireplace against which had been set a huge Greek jar filled with pinky-lavender rhododendron blooms. Over the marble mantel hung a painting of Greek columns like those in the photograph in her room at the hotel. Her host saw her eyes upon it.

"That is a scene from the acropolis of Lindos, here in Rhodes," he said. "One of the most beautiful spots in Greece. Those are the remaining columns of a temple of Athena. It is a place you will see while you are here."

Dad had explained the word "acropolis" before they left home. It did not refer only to the famous Acropolis in Athens. "Acro" meant "highest," and "polis" meant "city." So the acropolis was the high citadel of any Greek city. It was the place where fortifications had been built, and the great temples as well.

Down one side of the room were long bookshelves, and on the other side arched windows overlooked another part of the big garden. Her host indicated a Turkey-red armchair, and she sank into its enormous depths, feeling as though she were about to disappear. The old man seated himself in a dark leather chair beyond the expanse of a carved desk that had brass handles on all its drawers. Again there were art objects everywhere. Near Gale's chair was a handsome tile-topped table. On Mr. Castelis' desk was the sculptured head of a young boy, done in some reddish material. Beyond it stood a cruder figure in clay.

The old man touched the head rather sadly. "This

is one of my last attempts at sculpture. A portrait of Nicos when he was small.''

He turned the head for her to see, and she caught the sense of life he had captured in this portrait of his grandson. The boy looked as if he were about to laugh, to speak.

"I regret to say," the old man continued, "that the boy no longer looks at me like that. He is older now, and I fear that we do not always approve of each other."

This seemed an odd remark, and Gale made no attempt to answer it. "It must be wonderful to be an artist and have a real talent," she said a little enviously. "Did you always want to be a sculptor, Mr. Castelis?"

"I am complimented," he told her. "Perhaps I might have been an artist at one time had I not turned in another direction. But see here—we cannot have you calling me Mr. Castelis. That is much too formal, considering the fact that we are related by marriage. I suppose I could be considered your great-uncle. Or even a grandfather, if you prefer."

Gale answered on impulse. "My dad has three brothers, so I've lots of uncles. But I haven't a single grandfather."

He bent toward her chair and touched her hand lightly. His own hand was wrinkled and the veins showed along the back, yet his touch was both strong and gentle.

"Grandfather it shall be," he told her. "You must call me 'Grandfather Thanos.' I shall be honored. A man may never have too many granddaughters. Perhaps, since you are an American, you will help me to a better understanding of Tassoula, who is half American. In some ways Greeks are very much like Americans. But there are differences.''

Gale repeated his name softly to herself: "Grandfather Thanos." It did not seem so very strange.

The maid came through the door carrying a brass tray which she set on the nearby table with the tiled top. She smiled at Gale and went away.

"This is what we call *glyko*," the old man said. "It is something that is always served to a guest in a Greek home."

He showed her how to take a spoonful of the preserved fruit, dip it into the glass of cold water, then eat the sweet and sip the water. The maid had set out some squares of cake made from honey and nuts as well, and Gale ate with good appetite. Grandfather Thanos watched her, sipping only the water himself.

As she ate, he slid the tray aside a little on the table. "You may be interested to know that these tiles were made in our Pegasus Pottery factory. These ceramics have been produced by our family for three generations. I inherited the factory from my own father. Now, however, I am not well enough to go there every day, and a partner takes charge of running it."

Gale found herself wondering if the broken dish and the bits of tile she and Warren had found tucked so strangely among dancing clothes had also come from the Pegasus Pottery factory. If so, the fact gave her no answer to the puzzle.

She was finishing her second square of cake when someone came hurriedly through the door, only to stop in surprise at sight of Grandfather Thanos' guest. The newcomer was a tall boy of about fifteen, with blond hair and sea-green eyes. His face had a familiar look, and Gale realized that he resembled some of the handsome Greek statues she had seen yesterday in the museums of Athens. He no longer looked very much like the young head on his grandfather's desk.

He made a quick apology and had turned to leave when the old man stopped him. "Wait, Nicos. I wish you to meet your new American cousin. This is Gale Tyler, now visiting the Hermes."

The boy came toward her and held out a polite hand. "How do you do," he said. Gale could tell that he was not really interested in greeting her. His good-looking face wore a sullen expression, and his thoughts seemed to be upon other matters.

"Nicos is going to be the real artist of the family," his grandfather said. "I have every hope that he will make up for all the masterpieces I never created. Eh, Nicos, my boy?"

Instead of looking pleased, the boy scowled. "I have very little talent," he said flatly.

His grandfather shook his head reproachfully and gestured toward the small clay figure on the far side of his desk. "Fetch it here, Nicos, if you please. I would like to show your work to our young visitor."

For just a moment Gale thought the boy might refuse. Then he leaned over and picked the figure up in one hand and set it down on the tile-topped table so carelessly that only a quick movement by the old man saved it from falling.

"Do not provoke me, Nicos," his grandfather warned, and Gale was surprised at how stern and severe he could sound.

The boy apologized stiffly. "I'm sorry, sir." His

expression indicated that he disliked the small clay figure intensely.

Grandfather Thanos handed it to Gale, and she took it a little fearfully. It seemed to be a rather blurred impression of a dancer standing on crossed toes, her arms lowered before her body, the fingertips touching. There was a certain grace to the piece, but the sculptor had been indifferent about details.

"Our famous Lexine posed for Nicos when she was home for a visit last year," the old man said. "There is promise in the work, though he did not trouble to finish it. My grandson has only to apply himself to produce something fine."

Gale glanced at Nicos. The boy's eyes avoided his grandfather's; his handsome face was still sulky.

"I do not understand the young today," Grandfather Thanos said. "Tassoula, who needs only to become a good wife and mother when she grows up, has this ridiculous, futile drive to become something she can never be; while my grandson here, with talent in his fingertips, has no interest in what he might do with it." The old man looked at Gale. "Tell me, my young American friend, do you go against the wishes of your elders? In Greece it used to be that such a thing was unheard of."

Gale turned her gaze away from the handsome, sullen boy, who rather fascinated her, and blinked in embarrassment.

"I don't think anybody has any special plans for me," she said. "There's nothing I can do well."

The Greek boy made a faint sound, whether of scorn for her, or of resentment toward his grandfather, Gale could not tell. He said abruptly, "You will excuse me, please," and stalked from the room in a manner that warned them not to call him back.

In his leather chair Nicos' grandfather shook his head wearily. He looked tired and older than he had before. Gale wiped her fingers on a linen napkin and said she had better be going.

"Your visit has given me pleasure," the old man said, rousing himself to smile at her. "We must have Tassoula invite you for a proper visit. I have been in your country when I was young. There are many Greeks there. The people of our two countries have something of an affinity for each other."

He summoned the maid, and she led Gale downstairs and would have accompanied her to the gate. Just as they reached the path into the garden, however, a tall young figure stepped from beneath the shade of a plane tree.

"I will show you the way," Nicos said, and the maid left them.

He walked beside her in silence as they followed the winding drive, and she wondered why he wanted to do this if he did not choose to speak to her. A sidelong glance told her that he was still seething with anger against his grandfather, holding back his indignation with difficulty.

"I can find the gate by myself," she offered.

He looked at her then, his sea-green eyes flashing with some emotion she did not understand. "You will forgive me, please," he said in his rather formal English. "My thoughts were far away. I wished to see you alone in order to ask if you would deliver a message for me. A message to my cousin, Tassoula."

"Of course," Gale said readily. "When I see her,

that is. She hasn't been around much since we arrived. I think she's taking us to the old city this afternoon."

The boy nodded. "Then you will go to the museum, of course. But if you see her earlier, please tell her that all is arranged. Just those words—*'all is arranged.'*"

"I'll tell her," Gale promised.

They had reached the gate she had entered so uncertainly an hour before. But when she started to say good-by, Nicos bent toward her with an air of secrecy.

"Let no one else know of this message, please. It is very important to keep it a secret."

Gale wanted to say that she had seen the mirror signals that morning, but she did not quite dare. She merely agreed not to tell anyone except her cousin about the message.

He left her at the gate with a quick nod that seemed to dismiss her without further interest, and she walked back to the hotel feeling thoroughly bewildered. He was rather an arrogant boy, and she was not sure that she liked him. Nevertheless, he was interesting and he made her curious.

A block from the hotel she met Warren returning from the aquarium he had visited on the waterfront. She told him a little about her surprising visit to the Castelis house, but not about the secret message.

Warren was more interested in the odd-looking fish he had seen in the undersea tanks, and while he talked, Gale puzzled over Nicos. She could not help wondering at someone who had a talent and would not use it. If she had a gift for anything, she was sure she would never fight against it as Nicos was doing.

A strange boy—a very strange boy indeed.

🌿 🌿

4

In the City
of the Knights

At lunchtime Tassoula once more had an early meal with her mother and father and the employees, while Gale, Warren, and their mother dined when the dining room opened for guests. Thus there was no immediate opportunity to deliver Nicos' message. It seemed as though Tassoula was purposely avoiding her American cousins.

Right after lunch something happened that seemed peculiar to Gale. The entire town of Rhodes and all the people in it—indeed, all of Greece—retired for a long afternoon rest. The stores and public buildings closed, and office workers went home. Only a few tourists roamed about, ignoring the custom. For some two hours everything came to a halt.

Gale went to her room, but she did not feel like sleeping. She sat on the balcony looking out at nearby rooftops and across the sea to the Turkish mountains.

Dad had shown Warren and her a map of Greece before they left home, and she knew that Rhodes was one of twelve islands known as the Dodecanese—which meant twelve. It was situated at the foot of the Aegean Sea, the farthest island from the Greek mainland. It was larger than most of the Greek islands, though not so large as Crete. Its length was about fifty miles, and it was only a few miles across at its widest point. On the map its shape tapered at both ends, a little like the shape of a fish, and it was set at a diagonal with its nose pointing northeast, straight toward Anatolia in Turkey. The main town, Rhodes—or Rodos, as the Greeks called it—was where the Tylers were staying, right on the nose of the fish.

After a while, Gale grew tired of staring at what little of the town was visible from her balcony, and went into her room to stretch out on the bed and read. Her thoughts kept flitting from the page, however. So many odd things had happened since she got up that morning. Once she rolled over in bed and poked with her finger at the bright bits of tile in the ashtray. Part of the scarlet crab came into view, but it told her nothing.

In the end, the warm, drowsy afternoon began to have its effect, and she went sound asleep with the book open on her chest. It was Warren who wakened her by calling that everyone was ready for the visit to the old city.

Gale hurried downstairs to join Warren, Mother, and Tassoula. The Greek girl did not seem at all like the angry, rather fearful person Gale had seen that morning. She behaved rather shyly with Mother and seemed quite eager to please her. While she was carefully polite to Gale and Warren, she remained some-what distant, and it was plain that she still harbored resentment over the occurrences of the morning. Perhaps when she heard the message from Nicos she would forget that early meeting. But with Mother and Warren near, there was no chance for Gale to tell her.

As the four walked downtown together, Tassoula pointed out places of interest on the way. Near the waterfront stood a fine Government building with a long arcade of many arches making up the first floor. Farther on were more stone arches through which could be seen the open square of the market. Over-hanging balconies and the wooden latticework of Turkey were to be seen on some of the upstairs windows of houses along the way.

It was the old city of Rhodes toward which they walked. As they followed Mandraki, the wide water-front street, Warren was the first to see the towers and ancient walls rising ahead. The modern town had grown up and spread out around the walled town built by the Crusaders—the old city of the Knights of St. John of Jerusalem. The Knights had ruled the island for over two hundred years before being driven out by the Turks in 1522.

The road narrowed as it neared the walled city, running between the lower wall and the small, well-enclosed harbor. The Knights' city mounted the hill and was topped by the walls and towers of what Tassoula said was the Palace of the Grand Masters. It was the harbor, however, that held their attention for the moment.

Out across the inlet, where two thin arms of land almost met, allowing a narrow entrance into the harbor, stood the small squat fortress of St. Nicholas. Facing each other on either arm of land were two graceful bronze deer, placed there in honor of the deer that had once roamed the forested mountains of Rhodes. On the left arm of land was a row of windmills, their cloth arms turning slowly in a breeze.

"That's where the Colossus stood," Warren said eagerly, pointing toward the fortress.

Warren had been full of the story of the great Colossus of Rhodes ever since he had heard it. After one of the great sieges the conqueror Demetrius, admiring the spirit of the Rhodians, had turned over to them all the shattered, now useless equipment he had brought with him. He had suggested that money from this sale of scraps be used to erect a statue to commemorate the siege. A sculptor named Chares was supposed to have made the huge bronze figure of Helios (an earlier name for Apollo), and it had been known as one of the seven wonders of the ancient world. But it had stood for only fifty-six years before an earthquake threw it down, to lie for hundreds of years more in a shattered state, with no one to raise it up again.

"I wonder if there'd be a piece of the Colossus left anywhere?" Warren said thoughtfully.

Tassoula forgot to be distant and laughed aloud. "The story tells us that a merchant bought the pieces and carried them all away on nine hundred camels. No one knows what became of them. I'm sure there's not a bit of the statue left anywhere in Rhodes."

Warren's gaze moved to the stony beach below the sidewalk where they stood, and something new caught his attention.

"Look down there at the edge of the water," he said, pointing. "Those stone balls must have been thrown there by catapults hundreds of years ago."

Tassoula nodded. "Rhodes is full of them. There were so many sieges—all failing until the very last one."

Gale stared at the stony beach and saw that although all sorts of stones and boulders were scattered across pebbly sand, it was easy to pick out the catapult balls. They were of stone, but they had been shaped and rounded by human hands. Wet and brown and pockmarked, with the water lapping over them, they lay as they must have lain for centuries.

Gale had read stories of these ancient times, but they had always seemed too remote to be real. Now, suddenly, history no longer seemed so far away. It lay at her very feet. When she closed her eyes it was as if the sounds of the fighting, the tumult and shouting, the mighty crashing of a siege came to her down the years.

Warren forgot the shattered Colossus. "I'd sure like to have one of those balls to take home," he mused. "It would be almost like finding buried antiquities."

Mother smiled and shook her head. "Goodness, no! What would it do to our overweight baggage by air?"

"It is against the law to take any archaeological object out of Greece," Tassoula told him earnestly. "Not that those balls are so very valuable. There must be hundreds of them all around the town of Rhodes. They are not what you would called buried treasure."

"If I found something of value," Warren went on, dreaming again, "I wouldn't mind giving it up to the

Government. The important thing would be the discovering of something everyone else had missed, and possessing it myself for just a little while.''

Tassoula glanced at him curiously, and Gale noticed again what a pretty girl she was, with her brown eyes sparkling and a dimple that came and went in one cheek. But she was still not truly friendly; only polite.

''It's true,'' Tassoula said, ''that treasures are still being found all over Greece. Mostly through expeditions that are authorized to dig. But sometimes also by chance. Or because someone has an idea about a place in which to search. Many years ago my grandfather helped to excavate a fine marble piece near Camiros. I'll show it to you when we visit the museum this afternoon.''

They moved on toward two massive towers that guarded an entrance to the walled city. At once Warren was lost in admiration.

''This is the only Crusaders' city left intact in the world,'' he said raptly.

Tassoula agreed. ''This is true. And it is much the same as it was when the Knights lived here.''

Inside the walls the cobblestoned streets were narrow and twisting. As they crossed an open square, Gale saw old stone buildings rising on every hand. In many of the windows small panes of glass had been separated by wooden strips in the shape of a cross, so that the symbol of the Crusades looked down upon them from buildings all about.

Tassoula was bent on performing her duty as a guide. ''Perhaps you will wish to see the museum first?'' she suggested, gesturing toward a large building not far away.

"Fine—we'll start there," Mother said. "It used to be the Hospital of the Knights. The Knights Hospitalers, as they were called."

Before the deep arch of the entryway, Gale held back, hoping that Tassoula might let Mother and Warren go in ahead. Then the two girls would be alone and she could deliver Nicos' message. But Tassoula went in with Mother, and Gale followed the others through the Gothic arches. Beyond the entry a large courtyard opened, arched all about in blocks of stone, with the brilliant blue sky of Rhodes overhead. In one corner a flight of stone steps led to the upper galleries.

Across the courtyard a strange stone figure caught Gale's attention. It was a stone lion with huge hollows for eyes. It lounged upon a pedestal with more of the stone catapult balls piled on the floor nearby. Gale exclaimed and went toward it for a closer look. Tassoula left Warren and Mother to come with her.

"That's the lion your grandfather carved on the head of his cane, isn't it?" Gale asked.

Her cousin glanced at her in surprise. "How do you know that?"

"I visited him this morning," Gale said calmly. "He showed me all through his house. I met Nicos too. He gave me a message for you."

Tassoula stared in astonishment. Gale glanced over her shoulder, but Mother and Warren were looking at something on the other side of the court and she went on, speaking softly, quickly.

"Nicos said to tell you that *all is arranged*. He said

to use those very words and not let anyone else
know.''

Recovering from her surprise, Tassoula clasped her
hands dramatically. The message, it appeared, did not
please her.

''But nothing can be arranged now!'' she cried in
a low, furious voice. ''You and your brother have
spoiled everything. Why did you have to go to that
room? Why did you take those broken bits from the
leotard where I had hidden them? This afternoon I
returned to look—and they were gone!''

''Do you mean those pieces of tile with the red
crab in the pattern?''

''Ssh!'' Tassoula warned as Mother and Warren
came toward them.

There was no chance for Gale to explain that she
still had the bits of tile. Her cousin had turned her
back and was speaking with cheerful animation to
Mother about what was to be seen in the museum.

The stone steps that led to the gallery above had
no railing, and Gale walked carefully up the middle
as Tassoula led the way upstairs. Now the stone cor-
ridors and rooms of the Hospital of the Knights
opened around them. Tassoula led the way to a series
of small rooms, where the finest treasures of Rhodes
were kept. They paused before a lovely Venus, whose
outlines had been blurred by the long washing of
waves while she lay lost and forgotten at the bottom
of the sea. Gale was reminded a little of the statue of
Lexine that Nicos had modeled. That too was blurred
in its outlines. But with the slender Venus, one felt
that the details had once been there, while Nicos had
not bothered with them in the first place.

Mother remained to admire the Venus, and Gale wandered toward a case where a marble nymph knelt washing her hair. This was as beautiful and fascinating a statue as Gale had ever seen, and she called to Tassoula to come and tell her about it. Then, since no one else was paying attention, she stepped close to her cousin and whispered in her ear.

"Don't worry. The pieces of tile aren't lost. I have them. I'll give them to you when we go back to the hotel."

Tassoula sighed in relief. But she was still anxious, and not altogether forgiving.

"Please do not tell anyone about this," she murmured. "I am in great trouble." And she hurried back to Mother's side, as if she was afraid to be caught whispering her secret.

More puzzled than ever, Gale wandered on alone to the next room. There, occupying a place of honor against one wall, was a grouping in marble. The piece had fared badly over the centuries, and some of it was missing completely. A foot was gone, a hand, part of a body. Yet the effect was arresting and dramatic. There were several figures, one of them a woman dressed in a flowing robe, its folds beautifully executed in marble. She seemed to be reaching out in frightened supplication toward a monstrous creature that was part animal, part man, who appeared about to gallop off with a child clutched in its dreadful grasp. But though the marble piece was startling, it was not the thing that held Gale's attention, once she had noted the boy who stood looking at it.

Nicos' blond hair shone bright in the lighting of the room, his head was back, his gaze fixed in complete absorption upon the marble group before him. So great was his concentration that Gale hesitated to break in upon it. But she needed this chance to speak to him alone.

"Hello, Nicos," she said hesitantly.

He looked around at her and at once moved away from the marble piece as if to disclaim any interest in it.

"Good afternoon," he said. "Have you delivered my message to Tassoula?"

"I told her just a little while ago," Gale said. "But I think she's still worried about something."

Nicos made no comment. He seemed far away, as if lost in his own thoughts. To call him back, she motioned toward the marble group of figures.

"What does it mean? Is there a story about it?"

Nicos looked at the piece as if he had never seen it before. "I do not know," he said coldly.

Before Gale could say anything more, Tassoula came through the door from the next room and went to him eagerly.

"I have your message," she said. "Will it really be well, do you think?"

He smiled at her with kindly affection. It was the first time Gale had seen the sullen arrogance disappear, and she was reminded again of some handsome Greek sculpture out of the past.

"You are to come to the Pegasus day after tomorrow and bring the pieces," he told his cousin. "There will be no trouble. I have arranged it. I tried to signal to you in the usual place this morning, but you did not answer."

Tassoula glanced at Gale. "I could not. And when

I went to Grandfather's, you had gone out. But if the thing can be done, I am very happy."

The despondency seemed to fall away from her, and a gay exuberance took its place. As if she could not hold it in, she took two somewhat unbalanced ballet turns across the room in sheer happiness.

Nicos caught her arm, laughing. "Be careful," he warned. "You have a talent for breaking things, cousin, and this is not the place to indulge it."

Tassoula made a face at him, her eyes alight with mischief.

Mother and Warren came in from the next room, and there were introductions. The two boys regarded each other with interest, and Warren seemed pleased to meet this Greek cousin-by-marriage.

"I knew you would be coming here," Nicos said to Mother. "I have a message for you from my mother. She wishes you to visit her shop when you leave the museum. It is very close."

Mother said she would enjoy doing so and went on to view more sculpture in the next room. Nicos and Warren went with her, but once more Gale held back, her hand on Tassoula's arm.

"I don't understand what it's all about, but I'm glad everything is right again," she said eagerly. "We didn't mean to do the wrong thing—Warren and I."

Tassoula shrugged. "*Dem birasi.* That is what the Greeks always say—'it doesn't matter.' I should not have lost my temper. I did not think the broken pieces would be found in such a safe hiding place. But you Americans are always curious."

"You're part American," Gale said, prickling a little.

Tassoula looked at her for a moment as though she could not decide whether to be further annoyed. Then she smiled almost shyly.

"Greeks too are curious," she admitted. "Sometimes I think Greeks must be the most curious people in the whole world. And quick-tempered also."

Gale returned her smile in relief. At last they had begun to be friends. Wanting to keep her cousin there talking, she gestured toward the strange figure of woman and child and centaur.

"Is there a story about that statue? I asked Nicos, and he said he knew nothing about it."

"How strange," Tassoula said. "Nicos knows this piece very well. In fact, we have always been especially interested in it. This is the marble that my grandfather helped to find when he was a younger man. It is a very fine and famous piece. Perhaps by one of the great ancient sculptors. It is sad that it is badly damaged. But this is the way it was found at Camiros."

"What is Camiros?" Gale asked.

"You do not know?" Tassoula seemed surprised. "It is one of the three famous ancient cities of Rhodes—Camiros, Ialysos, and Lindos—all more than two thousand years old. They were known before the town of Rhodes was built, but they have crumbled to ruin. You will see them while you are here. Lindos is beautiful and exciting. Of Ialysos little remains, but it is on Mount Philerimos that there is a fine view. But I like Camiros best. Soon you must go there."

It was pleasant to have Tassoula over her indignation, and Gale's own spirits rose accordingly. She was still curious about many things, but the questions could wait. She would see much of Tassoula, and there would be time to clear everything up.

They went on through the museum, and Nicos took over the role of guide. He knew a great deal about the treasures of Rhodes and the history of ancient Greece. By the time they left the cold stone and drafty halls of the building and returned to the bright, warm light outside, Gale had gained a further respect for this tall, fair, Greek boy, whose grandfather, for some reason, did not approve of him.

The City of the Knights was a labyrinth of narrow, crooked streets, and while the main sections had a number of shops for tourists, the mass of ancient houses that climbed the hill were still much as they had been in the days of the Knights. As the little party walked along, Gale glimpsed courtyards and lovely gardens. Beyond the walls birds sang in the midst of shadowed stone, and now and then the scent of flowers reached her.

Their next stop was the shop of Mrs. Vera Casteli. Nicos' father, the older son of Grandfather Thanos, had died some years before, Tassoula told Gale, and Aunt Vera had decided to open this shop of fine handicrafts, though she still lived with Grandfather Thanos.

The shop was small and bright, with wide, open doorways, glass counters, and wall shelves from floor to ceiling. There was pottery from the Pegasus factory, handwoven skirts, lovely handbags, silver brooches and other jewelry. When the visitors stepped into the shop, Nicos' mother was waiting on a woman at the skirt counter. Clearly Nicos' fair hair came from his mother's side of the family. Aunt Vera was a true blonde and quite vivacious and pretty. She came at once to shake hands warmly with Mother, Gale, and Warren.

Gale, however, found herself staring at her customer. She would know that mound of peanut-butter hair anywhere. Mrs. Geneva Lambrou had put on stockings and high-heeled shoes, but otherwise she looked as she had at breakfast, with her blue-smudged eyes and towering wig. Gale was not sure why this absurd and bad-tempered little woman should give her a feeling of uneasiness, but she could not stop watching her. She noted the look of open dislike the woman had for herself and Warren. Then, as Mrs. Casteli spoke in English to the newcomers, it must have become evident that there was a relationship of some sort here. Mrs. Lambrou's hostile gaze flickered and changed subtly; her sullen mouth set itself in a more pleasant expression. Gale guessed that the woman was rearranging her thoughts in some fashion. She put down the skirt she was examining and moved from the counter as if she meant to intrude upon the introductions.

Nicos had stopped outside and had not entered with the others. Now, as he came up the single stone step into the shop, Mrs. Lambrou looked startled. For an instant it seemed to Gale that she had a desire to run away. She even made a step toward a side door. Then she seemed to reconsider. Instead of fleeing, she turned about boldly and faced the newcomer as if daring Nicos to say something. The boy gave her no more than a careless glance—he must have seen a good many strange-looking tourists—and remained uninterested. Only Gale was sharply aware of the

woman and of the fact that she seemed now to relax—
as if she had met some test and was no longer afraid.

A sudden memory came sharply back to Gale's
mind. The memory of a moment that very morning
when Mrs. Lambrou had stood on the balcony of the
Hotel Hermes looking out across rooftops toward a
big white house in a garden. Gale had heard the words
she had spoken, but the house had meant nothing to
her then. She remembered now that Geneva Lambrou
had said, ''The house of my enemy,'' and there had
been nothing in the least absurd about her as she
spoke the words.

5

Tassoula Confides

Mother and Aunt Vera seemed to take to each other at once, and when Mother mentioned that she had walked a lot in the museum and would be glad of a rest, the Greek woman brought a stool for her to sit on.

"Why not remain here?" she suggested. "Let the children walk about for a time while you visit here with me."

Mother accepted the invitation readily, and Tassoula said she would show Warren and Gale the famous Street of the Knights. At once Mrs. Lambrou hurried with her purchase. When the four young people stepped into the cobbled street, only Gale was aware of the woman's interest and knew that she was following them.

"I will leave you now," Nicos said when they paused outside the shop. "I have my motorbike nearby, and there is an errand I must do for my grand-father. Tassoula will show you all there is to be seen.''

To Warren's regret, Nicos left them, and Tassoula led the way toward the foot of the Knights' Street. A few paces behind, Geneva Lambrou teetered along on her stilted heels.

This was the street where the Knights themselves had lived, Tassoula explained. Sometimes it was called the Street of the Tongues, because so many languages had been spoken. Over some of the door-ways were still to be seen the coats-of-arms of the Knights, indicating the province or country from which they had come.

With part of her mind Gale listened to Tassoula, while another part remained aware of the woman who followed them.

Once she whispered to Tassoula. ''Don't look around now, but I think someone is on our trail.''

In spite of the warning, Tassoula looked around at once. ''Oh, yes—Mrs. Lambrou. She is staying at the hotel. Shall we invite her to join us? Perhaps she is lonely.''

This was hardly what Gale intended. ''She wasn't very nice at breakfast,'' Gale whispered. ''She com-plained to your mother because someone was jump-ing around in that room over her head. She was awfully mad about it.''

''I was *not* jumping around,'' Tassoula objected as vigorously as she had before, missing the whole point about Mrs. Lambrou. ''I was practicing.''

Warren had stopped to look more closely at a foun-tain in the middle of a small square. He rejoined them in time to hear Tassoula's words.

"What were you practicing for—the broad jump?" he asked, grinning. "That's what it sounded like. And what was that funny run down the hall for?"

Tassoula could get mad very fast. She threw Warren a look that was bright with resentment.

"I was dancing," she said. "I was doing ballet steps and leaps. I practice every day."

"But why the black cape and hood?" Warren persisted, paying no attention to her annoyance. "As if you were in disguise!"

"I was not in disguise!" Tassoula denied, her voice rising a little. "The cape is an old one belonging to Lexine. It makes me feel like Lexine when I wear it. My mother said I could have an empty room at the hotel all for myself for practicing. And it is a great advantage to run down the hall doing leaps. Now I will have to change the room because of Mrs. Lambrou."

Perhaps Mrs. Lambrou had heard her name, for she quickened her steps and caught up with them.

"May I come with you, please?" she asked, very friendly and pleasant now. "Since I am staying at the same hotel, and since I too have lived in America, I would like to meet these young people from that country."

"You've already met us," Warren said frankly. "We're the ones you thought were making all that noise in the room over your head this morning."

Mrs. Lambrou blinked her blue-shaded eyes at this direct approach. "I'm afraid I was irritable this morning. Often I have a bad temper when I first get up. But now we must all be friends, yes?"

"Of course," said Tassoula politely, thinking perhaps of her practicing and wanting to forestall further complaints.

"Sure—I guess so," Warren said without much enthusiasm. The way he stared at the tall wig was not altogether flattering.

Gale said nothing at all. The last thing she wanted was to be friendly with this odd, rather creepy little woman. She had a queer feeling that only she could see her as she really was—as if some special vision had been granted her. Tassoula was regarding her as a hotel guest to whom she must be polite, while Warren merely thought her silly. But to Gale there was something disturbing about Geneva Lambrou, and she had a feeling that they ought to be on guard against the woman.

"Lambrou is a Greek name," Tassoula said conversationally as they waited to let a small car and a motorbike pass in the narrow street. "But I think Geneva is not."

Mrs. Lambrou seemed happy to explain. She talked brightly and waved her hands to emphasize her words. "Lambrou is my husband's name. He was a Greek-American. My father was Greek, but my mother was French. Her name was Genevieve, so my parents gave me a variation of that name."

Tassoula remained politely interested. "What was your maiden name? Perhaps we know your family."

Mrs. Lambrou developed a sudden limp and seemed not to hear. Clinging to Warren's arm, she balanced on one high heel while she took off the other shoe, shaking it in the air. If there was a pebble inside, it made no sound as it fell out. She slipped her foot into the shoe and faced them all again, her pale lips smiling.

"It is very interesting that you are related to the Castelis family," she said. "I did not understand that the Americans were also related until just now in Mrs. Casteli's shop."

There seemed nothing to say to that, and Tassoula gestured toward the street they had just reached, speaking to Gale and Warren.

"Here is the Street of the Knights," she announced.

For the moment Gale forgot Mrs. Lambrou and her artificial friendliness. It was not a long street, but very narrow with a single-file sidewalk on each side. Its cobblestones marched straight up the hill toward the castle at the top. The stone fronts of the buildings on both sides were set flat against the street, and again there were many windows with the mark of the cross to be seen.

Mrs. Lambrou looked at the hill and shook her head. "If you are going up there, I am afraid I must leave you. My shoes are not right for walking. I believe I will find a taxi and return to the hotel. Another time perhaps we will go walking together."

"Of course," said Tassoula.

Still the little woman hesitated, as though she hated to tear herself from their company.

"Tell me," she said to the Greek girl. "It is your grandfather who lives in the big white house not far from the hotel?"

"Why, yes," said Tassoula. "How did you know?"

Mrs. Lambrou shook a roguish finger at her, but there was no amusement in her eyes. "I have lived in

Rhodes. I know many things. This house interests me. I have come here to take pictures of Rhodes for a book that may be published in America. I would like to photograph the Castelis' house. Would your grandfather permit this, do you think?''

''I don't know.'' Tassoula sounded doubtful. ''I could ask him.''

''We will wait a little while,'' said Mrs. Lambrou, very gay, very playful. ''Adieu for now. I will see you all at the hotel.''

She went hobbling off across the cobblestones, evidently in much better spirits than she had been that morning. Watching her go, Gale wondered if she might have misunderstood the word Mrs. Lambrou had used that morning on the balcony. If she merely wanted to photograph the house, it seemed unlikely that she would refer to its owner as an ''enemy.'' Perhaps the woman had spoken some foreign word, Gale thought.

Warren shook his head as Mrs. Lambrou went off. ''She's a nutty one. I wonder what she's up to?''

''We must not be unkind,'' Tassoula said gently. ''I heard my mother say that she is very young. Perhaps she has no one to tell her that her own hair is prettier than a wig, and that it is not good taste to put so very much blue coloring on the eyes.''

Gale had nothing to add to their comments. At least Mrs. Lambrou had changed her mind about coming with them, and they could go on by themselves. She must stop feeling uneasy and suspicious about her.

Although the distance up the hill was not great, there were stops to be made along the way and they moved slowly. Here and there arched openings to side streets invited them, and they had to explore. The side streets were even narrower than the Street of the Knights, and these alleys zigzagged off in almost every direction. Beyond the open doorways they passed were mysterious courtyards and more than once they stepped through an opening to look at the hidden gardens inside.

At last they moved beneath stone arches and out into the open at the top of the hill where an open square spread before the castle gates. Now they could see the high, square, central tower of the castle, the crenelated walls and battlements. Two huge round towers guarded the gateway, and Tassoula gestured toward the entrance.

"Come, we will go inside the castle. There is a small charge. I will pay—today you are my guests."

She gave the drachmas to the attendant at the gate, and they went through into the great lower hall of the Grand Masters' Palace. Tassoula explained that the building had been in bad repair, and when the Italians had occupied the island during World War II, they had rebuilt, restored, and refurnished it. The restoration did not belong entirely to the period of the Knights, but it was all very rich and grand and beautiful inside.

Gale had a sense of awe as they walked about. It was difficult to think of herself moving through a medieval castle where knights of the Crusades had once lived. Warren's interest was more practical. He began to examine the stone walls, looking for parts that belonged to the original castle, and parts that were of more recent construction. Before long he had wandered off by himself, as he often liked to do. Gale

and Tassoula climbed the grand staircase together and
wandered about as they pleased.

"Do you come here often?" Gale asked.

Again Tassoula gave her light shrug. "Only when
there are visitors who wish to see the palace. My
grandfather says we Greeks are the last to visit our
museums and ancient places these days. If it were not
for our guests, some of us might forget they exist. He
becomes angry about this. He is annoyed with my
father, who gives all his time to the hotel, or to other
business projects, and is not interested in the ancient
things."

"Nicos seems interested," Gale said.

"Yes and no." Tassoula hesitated. "He has great
interest in all that Grandfather has taught him of ancient matters. But he does not wish to become what
Grandfather wishes him to be—a sculptor, or an artist."

"What does Nicos want to be?" Gale asked.

"This is difficult to explain." Again there was hesitation in Tassoula's manner. "Let us speak of other
things. It makes me sad to see my grandfather and
my cousin opposing each other. I love them both very
much."

Once more Gale stemmed her questions and her
growing curiosity.

The rooms of the castle were hung with paintings
and rich draperies. The floors were the fine parquetry
the Italians had set down, and there were Oriental
rugs, roped off so that one did not walk upon them.

Window embrasures flung light into these upper
rooms, and Gale stopped before one of the windows,
entranced. Stone steps, old and worn by many feet,

led to two stone seats facing each other beside the window.

"I'd like to sit in one of those places," Gale said.

Tassoula was willing, and they took opposite seats and leaned their elbows on the deep stone sill, looking out upon the old city. Now Gale could see the close-packed roofs of the houses, with twisting streets between. The cross and dome of a Greek church and the tall minaret and dome of a Turkish mosque rose above the roofs. The towers and walls of the palace belonged to another age, another time, and the modern world seemed far away.

It was Tassoula who broke the spell. She had been watching Gale instead of the view she knew so well. She reached out with a light hand to touch the knee of her American cousin.

"Is there something you wish to be when you grow up?" she asked.

Startled, Gale brought herself back from historic times. "Nothing special, I'm afraid," she said. "I'm not a bit like my sister Audrey. Audrey can do everything well. She can paint and write and dance and sing. Everyone knows she will do something important. But not me. Anyway, Mother and Dad say there isn't any rush."

Tassoula nodded. "Most Greek girls wish to marry and have a nice house and many children. Perhaps for me, also—but later, much later. First I wish to be like Lexine."

There was a glow in her eyes as she spoke, and her cheeks were flushed with the eagerness of her thoughts. Gale listened in surprise as she went on.

"This is why I work at my dancing. This is why I

practice every day. Because the most wonderful thing I can imagine would be to have the grace, the talent, the beauty of my sister Lexine.''

If Lexine was any prettier than Tassoula, she must indeed be a great beauty, Gale thought. Somehow her cousin's fervent desire to follow in the footsteps of her famous sister made Gale feel uncomfortable.

''I'm just the opposite,'' she admitted. ''When somebody asks me if I'm going to be like my wonderful sister, I dig in my heels and tell them I only want to be me.''

Tassoula looked at her almost pityingly. ''How sad to have no ambition,'' she said.

''Maybe there are different kinds of ambition,'' Gale said. ''How can I know what I really want when I haven't even found out who I am yet?''

''What do you mean?'' Tassoula asked. ''You are Gale Tyler. This you know very well.''

Gale shook her head. ''Who is Gale Tyler? Once I asked my dad that right out. Warren laughed his head off, but Dad said it was a sensible question and that finding who we are inside ourselves is what growing up is all about. He said when I began to understand the feelings of other people, I'd also find out about me. I'm not sure I know what he meant, but I do know I don't want to be another Audrey. I only want to be someone myself. Someone I can like. Sometimes I don't like myself very much at all.''

Clearly none of this made much sense to Tassoula, and Gale could not blame her, since she herself was still groping for an answer.

''I shall be like Lexine,'' her cousin went on

dreamily. She moved a foot, pointing her toe, and raised one hand in a fleeting gesture, as if she were dancing.

"Your grandfather doesn't want you to be a dancer, does he?" Gale said, remembering the words Grandfather Thanos had spoken.

Tassoula came back to earth with an almost audible thud. "Grandfather understands nothing at all about young people! He is old and he has forgotten. Nicos and I are young."

"I liked your grandfather a lot," Gale said, feeling a sudden need to defend the old man. "I had a feeling that he understood very well about my being young, and that he did not mind."

Tassoula tossed her head, and dark curls trembled about her forehead. "Of course! It is not the same for you. There is nothing he expects of you. It does not matter to him what you do with yourself. For us— for Nicos and me—he wants to make plans. He wants to live our lives for us because—because—" she broke off, and Gale saw to her dismay that there were tears in Tassoula's eyes.

The Greek girl jumped down from the embrasure and beckoned. "Come, let us go back to the shop and find your mother. Then we can return to the hotel, and you will give me the pieces of tile you removed from the leotard. That is the only important thing now, and I must have them soon."

Gale too jumped down from the stone seat and stood beside her cousin. The other girl's moods changed so quickly that it was hard to keep up with her. But Gale was willing enough to return to the hotel for the pieces of tile. Perhaps then Tassoula would be willing to clear up the mystery of what was going on.

6

The Odd Ways of Geneva Lambrou

Together the girls went searching for Warren and found him without difficulty. He was ready enough to stop sight-seeing for today and return to the hotel. This Italian restoration was no place, he had decided, to find buried antiquities.

They hurried down the hill to the shop, where Mother was rested and waiting for them. Aunt Vera had an invitation for Warren and Gale.

"Tassoula's grandfather has telephoned and asked me to invite you both to come to the house tomorrow afternoon and spend the night. Tassoula will come with you, and of course Nicos will be there."

The invitation was accepted with pleasure, and a time was set. Then they said good-by and walked back to the hotel. There Tassoula ran upstairs ahead of Gale, as if she could not wait to get those bits of tile safely into her hands.

"Where have you put them?" she demanded the moment she was in Gale's room.

"Right over here in the ashtray," Gale said and hurried across the room.

The ashtray itself was Pegasus pottery. It sat upon the bed table, terra cotta in color, large, shallow, and completely empty. For a moment Gale stared at it in disbelief.

"I put the pieces right there," she said. "The ashtray was the right size to hold them. They were still there this afternoon before I went out. Who in the world—"

"The maid!" Tassoula cried, and Gale remembered that she was staying in a hotel where someone was apt to come into one's room and straighten up at any time.

"I'll ring for her," Gale said and started toward the bell.

Tassoula was ahead of her. She pulled open the door and shouted a name in a voice that could be heard all along the echoing hallway and down the stairs to the next floor. Probably a good idea, Gale thought. The maids did not always come at once when you rang.

In a moment a startled young Greek girl appeared on the stairs and came running toward Tassoula. There was a rapid-fire exchange in Greek. The girl ran across to the ash tray and stared at it. Then she turned it upside down, illustrating, and waved a hand toward the stairs. Tassoula sent her away, tragic and despairing.

"She had been told to empty all ash trays," Tassoula said. "So that is what she has done. The broken pieces of tile have been thrown out in the rubbish. There is no chance to recover them now." Tassoula dropped down on the bed and covered her face with her hands. "What am I to do, what am I to do?"

Feeling thoroughly guilty and unhappy, Gale sat beside her. "I'm awfully sorry. Is—is there any way I can help? I don't understand why something that is broken is so important, but—"

"It is the only one. The only one—and there is no pattern!" Tassoula wailed. She took her hands from her face and looked at Gale, her eyes swimming with tears. "It is not your fault. You could not know. If I had not been so angry, I could have recovered the pieces before you took them away. Grandfather will never forgive me for this." She closed her eyes and shivered dramatically. "I do not know what he will do."

With an effort she seemed to stem her emotions in full tide and even managed to smile at Gale.

"Do not be unhappy," she said. "Do not blame yourself. I will talk to Nicos. Perhaps he will think of something. And tomorrow you will come to visit with me as we have planned."

She jumped up and ran out of the room before Gale could think of anything to say. When her cousin had gone, Gale picked up the ashtray and stared at it for a moment, as though it might give her the answer to this latest puzzle. Clearly Tassoula had broken something important, and Nicos was trying to help her to replace it. Without the original pieces, this would apparently be difficult. But that Tassoula should be so distraught and despairing about such an accident was hard to understand.

As she put the ashtray down and stepped away from the bed table, her toe struck something that skittered away on the floor. At once she knelt and reached under the bed to pick up a small bit of broken tile. On the glazed side it showed a part of the crab's claw; on the other side a tiny wing was imprinted in the unglazed clay. She turned the ashtray over and compared the two. Yes, this wing must belong to the trademark of all Pegasus pottery—a little winged horse in flight.

But why all the fuss? Why couldn't Nicos have a small tile like this made even though the original pieces were gone? There was still something puzzling here. Gale dropped the bit of tile into her pocket and went to see what Warren was doing.

She found him leaning on the balcony rail, looking down into the street in front of the hotel.

"There's our peculiar friend," he said to Gale.

In the street Geneva Lambrou was talking to the desk clerk from the hotel, and the subject of the conversation seemed to be a medium-sized car that stood at the curb.

"Looks like an English car," Warren said. "Let's go down and see."

Gale had no special desire to be near Mrs. Lambrou, but it would be something to take her mind off Tassoula and the trouble she was in.

They ran downstairs and arrived just as Mrs. Lambrou got into the car. She saw them and presented her somewhat tight smile.

"Would you like to come for a ride in my car?" she asked.

"Sure," Warren said without hesitation. "Have you bought it for your own?"

The woman shook her head, the wig barely grazing the low roof of the car. "I am renting it from the hotel for my stay in Rhodes. If you would like a short ride with me, ask your mother, and then we will go."

Gale was not sure she wanted to go riding with Mrs. Lambrou, but Warren had gone off to get permission, and when he came back there was nothing else to do. Gale got into the middle in the front seat, with Warren beside her. Sitting close to Geneva Lambrou, the scent of geraniums was once more overpowering and she held her finger under her nose to keep from sneezing.

Warren asked questions about the car, and Mrs. Lambrou, who seemed quite at ease as a driver, put it into gear and they drove down the street.

At the waterfront they turned and followed the highway that led out of town, skirting the bright blue Aegean Sea. It would have seemed a more pleasant drive to Gale if it had not been for the woman at the wheel. Warren was interested mainly in the car and seemed to sense none of what Gale continued to feel about this woman.

At length Mrs. Lambrou found a place to turn the car about and they headed back to town.

"You must come with me for a longer trip sometime soon," she said. "Your mother too. Perhaps we will go to Camiros. Or to Lindos. I was born in Lindos. I have a brother there."

"Do you have a large family?" Gale asked, for want of anything better to say.

For a few moments there was no answer, and when

Gale stole a look at the woman beside her, she was startled by the queer, cold look of her face.

"My parents are dead," she told them. "My sister also. My parents were very old, but my sister was young. She did not need to die."

After that no one said anything until they were back in Rhodes. The cold, white look was still on Mrs. Lambrou's face, and she made no further attempt at light conversation.

When they reached the street that led toward the hotel, she drove on and took another turning. Then she slowed the car and went at a snail's pace beside the high stone wall that hid a garden. With a start, Gale recognized where they were. This was the house of Grandfather Thanos—the house of the Castelis family.

Mrs. Lambrou spoke suddenly. "There is the boy— in the gateway speaking with a gardener. We will drive past so that you may wave to him, yes?"

When Nicos did not look up from his conversation, Mrs. Lambrou touched the horn lightly. He turned his head and saw them, and Warren called, "Hello!" and waved. Gale said nothing, watching the queerly eager way in which Mrs. Lambrou stared at Nicos. The Greek boy raised a hand in greeting. Then he saw Mrs. Lambrou and gave her a sudden, long, hard look. He did not speak, however, but returned his attention to the gardener.

Mrs. Lambrou stepped on the gas with a suddenness that jerked the car and betrayed her irritation. "He tries to be superior—that one. Like the old man, his grandfather. He does not know what it is to be friendly." Then she must have become aware of the way Gale was staring at her, for she seemed to rearrange her expression deliberately and managed a wide, stiff smile, as if to soften the effect of the words she had spoken.

Gale was glad to return to the hotel. Warren got out quickly, and before she followed him Gale turned to their driver, making an effort to be polite.

"Thank you for the ride, Mrs. Lambrou," she said.

"Mrs. Lambrou!" that lady echoed playfully. "You make me feel very old. I was young like you not long ago. Please—you will call me Geneva. And I will call you Gale and Warren. Then we will all be good friends."

Warren, waiting for Gale on the sidewalk, threw her a look that promised nothing. Mrs. Lambrou put out a thin hand and clasped Gale by the wrist. Her fingers felt unpleasantly hot, as though she was excited about something.

"Come now—you must say it. Not 'thank you, Mrs. Lambrou,' but 'thank you, Geneva.' "

Gale repeated the words reluctantly, wanting only to have Mrs. Lambrou release her hand. Warren ran up the steps, and Gale was glad to hurry after him.

"I told you she was nutty," he said as Gale caught up with him. "Nutty as a pistachio."

Gale could only agree.

At dinner that night they discussed Mrs. Lambrou. Since Mother was waiting till later to eat with Aunt Marjorie and her husband, and Tassoula had gone to her grandfather's, they were alone and could speak freely. While Warren did not like Geneva Lambrou, he was less inclined than Gale to worry about her.

"Even if she is nutty, it's in a harmless sort of way," he said.

Gale disagreed. "I'm not so sure she's harmless. Why is she so interested in the Castelis family? I think that stuff about photographing the house is just some sort of excuse. Maybe we shouldn't be too friendly with her."

"Suits me fine," Warren said. "If she's got a private feud going on, I don't want to get mixed up in it. But she's not big enough to hurt a flea. Don't worry about her."

Warren's cheerful good sense made Gale feel a little better. Still, she could not put Mrs. Lambrou entirely from her mind.

The next day was Sunday, and Aunt Marjorie invited her guests to visit the Greek church that she attended with her husband and his family. The church was a very old one, built in the typical Greek way, with a high dome, elaborately decorated on the inside. The service was very different from what Gale was accustomed to at home, and since not a word was spoken in English, she felt a little lost.

In the afternoon, when lunch and the usual rest period was over, Aunt Marjorie accompanied Gale and Warren to Grandfather Thanos' house. They had been asked to have tea with him at four thirty in his study. The two Americans were to stay for dinner and spend the night. These days Tassoula seemed to alternate between living at the hotel and in her own room at her grandfather's house. Tonight Gale would stay with her in the big house.

They arrived early, since Aunt Marjorie had some things she wanted to do, and Nicos took Warren into the garden to show him around, while Gale went with Tassoula to her room.

It was a large room at one side of the house, its windows overlooking a section of the garden. The ceiling was very high, and there was a spaciousness that made it seem cool in spite of the warmth of the afternoon.

One of the first things to catch Gale's eye was a solid block of glossy photographs tacked up on one wall. They were all poses of Lexine in various dancing roles, some alone, some with a partner. Tassoula came to Gale's side, her expression wistful as they looked at the pictures together.

"See her there as the Swan Queen, with her little winged cap and feathery tutu," Tassoula said. "She's so beautiful in that dance—it makes me cry to see her."

Gale glanced from her cousin's rapt expression back to the pictures. Lexine had a rather bony face, with high cheekbones and deep-set eyes. It did not seem to Gale that she was nearly so pretty as her younger sister. But she did not dare say this to Tassoula, who stared at the photographs, blinded by love and admiration.

Gale turned from the dancing figures to look about the room. The bed was huge and old-fashioned, with four carved posters and a canopy overhead. On a massive bureau, made from some fine dark wood, stood what Gale recognized as an evzone doll. The evzones were the soldiers of the royal guard, and she had seen them on duty before the palace, day before yesterday, in Athens. Their costume was made up of short stiff skirts like petticoats, which stuck out rather like a dancer's tutu. The doll's blouse was white with long full sleeves, a scarf was wound about its head, and an embroidered vest and bright red sash completed the costume. Beneath the billowy skirts the evzone wore long white tights, with tasseled garters above the knees, and red shoes that turned up and ended in big black pompons on the toes.

The dress had seemed surprising to Gale's unaccustomed eyes, but she knew these soldiers were known to be great fighters and there was nothing feminine-looking about them in spite of their skirts.

Tassoula saw her interest in the doll. "Nicos' mother gave it to me on my last name day. Fighters used to dress like that in the mountains of Greece. It is a great honor to be an evzone."

Except for a handwoven rug before a cushioned window seat and another beside the bed, the floor of the room was carpetless and cool. All the furniture seemed to have been pushed back against the walls, leaving a large free expanse in the middle of the floor.

"I should think this would be a wonderful room for dancing," Gale said. "Do you practice here when you're at home?"

Tassoula shook her head and plumped herself among the cushions on a wide window seat. "I used to. But now my grandfather has forbidden me to dance in this house. He has stopped my lessons and has told my father that I am to have no more."

A little shocked, Gale joined her cousin in the big window. "But that's terrible if you really want to dance! He doesn't seem like such an unkind person. Did your grandfather try to stop Lexine too?"

"Lexine always did whatever she wished," Tassoula said, sounding a little resentful. "Grandfather said it was her American blood coming out and that she was not a proper Greek woman. But now he is very proud of her. Yet no one will believe that I can be a dancer too. Mother says I am to dance if I wish—and I may do so on the fourth floor of the hotel, since it is empty. But I know she doesn't take me seriously. Everyone is waiting for me to outgrow this wish."

"Are you a good dancer?" Gale asked. "Can you tell whether or not you are?"

Tassoula flung up her hands in a despairing gesture. "How can I be a good dancer when everyone opposes me and Grandfather will not let me have my chance? But I will show them! I am working hard to perfect myself. When Lexine comes home she will see that I have improved. She will be on my side. Sometimes I wish I could go to America. It is different for you in America. Women may do as they like."

"Can't they in Greece?"

"Not altogether," Tassoula said. "Though some things are changing. Our parents are very strict with girls. Our families think it is better for a Greek girl to marry and have a family. Most of my friends wish only this. But for me—"

Tassoula closed her eyes and turned her back upon the sunny, green world of the garden. There was a dreaming in her voice as she continued.

"I can see how it would be. I can imagine myself on a great empty stage—with only me in the center. With the spotlight upon only me. When the swan dies at the end, the audience would weep. And how they would applaud me—just as they applaud Lexine."

Gale regarded her cousin with sympathy. She knew

what Tassoula meant by her imaginings. She herself
had dreamed of doing a drawing so perfect that everyone would exclaim over it. Or writing a story that
would be published in a book that everyone would
read and praise. Or perhaps just making a graduation
speech as fine as the one Audrey had made. It was
always fun to pretend to be famous and important and
beautiful. But in the end she always opened her eyes
and looked at herself in a mirror. And then she had
the good sense to laugh. Because she doubted that
she would be any of these things, and she did not
really care.

The dreamy look vanished from Tassoula's face and
she opened her eyes. "Someday I will *be* somebody!
Somebody important and successful and famous. You
should see the way everyone looks at Lexine and bows
to her wishes and consults her. Even Grandfather. But
me—always I am in trouble. Always I break things. I
stumble and I am clumsy."

"So far," Gale said, "I haven't seen you break
anything, or stumble even once, and you certainly
aren't clumsy."

"Ah, if you only knew!" Tassoula cried and rolled
her eyes dramatically heavenward.

A tap on the door by the maid summoned them to
tea in Grandfather Thanos' study, and Gale was happy
to draw Tassoula away from her despairing mood.

Thanos Castelis awaited them in his deep leather
armchair. He rose courteously when they came to the
door, and invited them in. A tea table had been spread
with an embroidered linen cloth, and the teacups were
of a delicate translucent china. Nicos and Warren appeared from the garden, and they all found chairs and

waited for Aunt Marjorie to join them and pour the tea.

Grandfather Thanos greeted Gale as if he considered her an old friend, and she might have felt at home with him at once if it had not been for the restraint that seemed to rest upon Nicos and Tassoula. Nicos seemed sullen again, almost disapproving in his attitude toward his grandfather, while Tassoula was ill at ease and even a little fearful, as if she expected to drop her teacup. Grandfather questioned Gale's brother about his interests, and Warren seemed the most comfortable one in the room.

Grandfather Thanos was delighted with his interest in ancient Greece and was talking to him about Rhodes when Aunt Marjorie came into the room with a little rush, apologizing for being late.

"The strangest thing has happened," she said. "I wanted to get out that Pegasus box, so I could show Warren and Gale the lovely present the family is going to give Lexine. But the box isn't there."

Grandfather's bushy eyebrows, so dark in contrast to his nearly white hair, drew down in a frown. "But of course the box is there. I gave orders that it was to be placed in Lexine's room—where she will find it when she comes home."

Aunt Marjorie seated herself before the tea table and began to pour amber tea into fragile cups and pass them around.

"I looked everywhere," she said. "Even under the bed. The box isn't there. So I asked the servants. The garden boy thought he knew something and went off to look."

"I do not understand this," Grandfather Thanos

said and looked at Nicos and Tassoula. "Have you any knowledge of this matter?"

Tassoula's gaze was fixed anxiously on Nicos, but before he could answer, the garden boy came to the door. Grandfather told him to enter, and he came in carrying a large wooden box. Stamped on its side Gale saw the emblem of the Pegasus' winged horse.

Grandfather Thanos spoke to the boy rapidly in Greek, and he answered in the same language.

"This appears to be the box," the old man said to Aunt Marjorie. "Petros found it hidden behind some things in the tool shed. But it was empty. I do not understand the meaning of this. Nicos, Tassoula, you have not answered me."

Nicos stared at the oriental pattern of the carpet at his feet as though he had not heard the words. Tassoula flushed a bright red. Neither volunteered any information, though Grandfather Thanos' keen eyes rested upon them thoughtfully.

In Gale's mind there was a sudden clear picture of the broken pieces of a tile with a scarlet crab painted upon it. But so small a tile could not fill so large a box. If there were others, what had happened to them?

When neither of his grandchildren spoke, Grandfather Thanos addressed them sternly. "We will let the matter pass for now and return to it at another time when we do not have guests. There is something here I do not understand."

The garden boy went away, and the bright color faded from Tassoula's face. She threw a quick, almost helpless glance at Nicos, who did not look at her at all. Then, as if she sought to change the tense, emotion-charged climate of the room, sought to appease her grandfather, she put down her teacup and went to get the small clay figure of Lexine that Nicos had made.

"Have you seen this?" she asked Gale and started toward her before Gale could answer that she had.

Perhaps Tassoula was still nervous, perhaps she was so intent upon the figure in her hands that she did not watch where she put her feet. As she neared Gale, her toe caught in a fold of carpet, so that she stumbled and nearly fell. The clay figure was juggled precariously in her hands, but somehow she managed to catch it before it slipped from her grasp.

Grandfather Thanos lost his temper. "Set it down!" he roared. "Set it down at once!"

Tassoula's hands were shaking as she set the figure upon the tile-topped table, and Gale saw the alarm in her eyes.

"If you break one more thing, Tassoula—" her grandfather paused and tried to continue more calmly. "This clumsiness must stop. How do you think you can be a dancer when you cannot manage your own feet even in walking? In any case, one Lexine in a family is enough."

The tears welled in Tassoula's eyes and spilled over. She burst into soft sobs, weeping into her hands. At once Nicos was at her side.

"Do not cry, little one," he said gently. "It would not matter in the least if the clay figure were broken. It was not your fault that the rug had a wrinkle and tripped you."

Tassoula wept on, and Aunt Marjorie went to put an arm comfortingly about her daughter. The look she threw Grandfather Thanos was one of pure American rebellion, but she checked herself from speaking her mind at that moment.

Nicos turned angrily to his grandfather, and the two stared at each other for a long, challenging moment. Then Nicos did a dreadful and astonishing thing.

With one finger he reached out and pushed at the clay figure of Lexine. It fell over upon the tiles of the table with a little crash and shattered into several pieces.

The old man sat as if he were made of stone. Only Aunt Marjorie's shocked gasp broke the sudden stillness of the room. Gale hardly dared to breathe, and even Tassoula checked her sobs in terror. At length Grandfather Thanos stirred and spoke to his grandson.

"Why did you do that?"

Nicos faced him, very straight and defiant, though he had turned quite pale. "The figure was not well made. Perhaps one Thanos Castelis in a family is also enough." Thereupon he turned his back on the old man and addressed himself courteously to Warren. "Would you like to come with me?" he invited and went out of the room, leaving a frightened silence behind him.

❧ ❧

7

Discovery!

Grandfather Thanos sat on, staring without expression at the broken pieces of the little clay figure. When she could bear it no longer, Tassoula jumped up and fled from the room in the wake of her cousin. With an apologetic smile for Gale, Aunt Marjorie slipped from her chair and went after her daughter.

Gale found herself wondering whether to go or to stay. In spite of the angry way in which he had spoken to Tassoula, the old man looked so sad and lonely, with everyone deserting, that she somehow felt sorry for him. Reluctant to leave him as the others had, yet unable to sit in this dreadful silence doing nothing, Gale chose the only course of action that occurred to her. She bent over the broken pieces on the table and began to put them together, as she had done with the bits of broken tile. It was more difficult in this case, for the dry clay had crumbled and was brittle to her touch.

"Perhaps it can be mended," she said softly.

"It is of no importance." There was a harsh note in the old man's voice. "The clay was never baked— it could not last. There is a wastebasket beneath my desk. Put the pieces into it, please."

So directed, she gathered up the crumbling bits that had once been a crude figure of Lexine, and did as he bade. Behind her the old man's voice went on, almost as though he spoke to himself.

"I do not understand what has come about between Nicos and me. When he was young—" Grandfather Thanos gestured toward the head he had modeled of the little boy, Nicos, "—there was great love between us. I made fine plans for my grandson, and he seemed to welcome my love and my belief in him. Even a year ago we were friends, even though he had rejected my ambition for him. Now it is as though he hated me. Yet I have wanted nothing for him except the best in life."

He paused, watching Gale as she returned to her chair. Then he went on.

"Always I have taught Nicos to love and respect the ancient things. He is filled with knowledge of them. When he was small he seemed to have the gift of creation in his own hands. If only he would work, he could contribute something fine to modern Greece. Yet he opposes me, as I never opposed my own father."

He seemed to expect some response from her, and Gale blinked and spoke in a low, uncertain voice.

"Did you want to be what your father wanted you to be?"

The old man spread his hands before him, palms down, and stared at them. They were the hands of age, with swollen joints and brown patches on the skin; yet they looked strong and sensitive.

"Once these hands held the power," he said. "I could have used them to strike to the heart of marble and find the beauty imprisoned there. But my father did not wish this for me. His thoughts were given to the growth of the Pegasus factory. He needed me there. Since I was an obedient son, I did as my father wished. My elder son, Nicos' father, had no talent. He cared nothing for clay or marble, though he cared deeply for Greece. He died fighting for our country in the war. The younger son, Alexandros, is interested only in business. Thus all my hopes were turned upon Nicos. I determined that if he showed the gift, he should have the opportunity to be a sculptor I could never become. I would have done all I could to help and encourage him. But Nicos chooses to turn his back upon his gifts, and he looks at me now with anger in his heart."

Again Gale spoke hesitantly. "Nicos says the clay figure wasn't very good."

"That is true. But he had only to go on from there, to persist, to learn. The figure was a beginning."

"Like Tassoula's dancing is a beginning?" Gale asked.

The old man threw her a quick look and his smile was wry. "There is, perhaps, a similarity. Strange that in one child ambition should burn so high, and in another not at all." He roused himself and reached for the lion-headed cane beside his chair. "Come now, my young friend—I have bored you with my problems long enough. These are not matters for you to trouble about. I should not have shouted at Tassoula. We Greeks are excitable, but my manners were bad. I apologize to you as a guest. I will apologize to my granddaughter later. Perhaps now it will be better if you go and comfort her."

Eager to escape, Gale slipped from her chair and started toward the door. As she reached it, he spoke again.

"Do you like to read, my young friend?"

"Oh, yes," Gale said quickly.

He waved a hand toward the bookshelves behind him. "Then you must feel free to come to this room at any time to borrow books during your stay in Rhodes. I have many books in this section near the window that are in English. Many of them are about Greece. Perhaps you will enjoy learning more about the country you are visiting.

"Thank you," Gale told him. And then because there still seemed something touchingly lonely about the tall figure leaning on his cane, she added softly, "Thank you, Grandfather Thanos."

His smile rewarded her, and she went out of the room feeling a little better.

On her way down the hall she met Aunt Marjorie coming out of Tassoula's room.

"How is he?" her aunt asked, nodding toward the study.

"I think he's not angry any more," Gale said. "He's sorry that he shouted at Tassoula."

"He shouldn't have spoken to her like that, it's

true. But Nicos behaved badly and upset him even more. About a year ago Mr. Castelis was very ill and close to death. He has recovered well, but we try not to anger or excite him these days. I don't know what this mystery is about Lexine's gift disappearing, but Tassoula has asked me not to push it any farther right now. Since she assures me that the tiles aren't lost, perhaps I'll simply tell Grandfather that all is well, so he won't worry about the matter. If you like, you can go visit Tassoula now. I think your company will help."

Gale was not sure that it would, but she went to knock on her cousin's door and was surprised at the bright "Come in!" that greeted her.

As she entered the room, Gale saw that Tassoula had quenched her tears and washed her face. Her cousin was very busy with water colors, brushes, and paper that she had set out upon a table near a window.

"Do you like to paint?" she asked Gale, glancing around at her cheerfully.

Astonished by this sudden change, Gale nodded. "I guess so. Your grandfather is sorry he shouted at you. He said he would apologize to you later."

With a quick gesture, Tassoula put her hands over her ears. "I don't want to talk about it. Or think about it either. Now that the empty box has been found, I don't know what will happen. Nicos says not to worry. And my mother says she will put Grandfather off for a while longer. Tomorrow after school we will go to the Pegasus and see if there is anything to be done. Perhaps you and your brother can come too, and we will show you how pottery is made. But now I will paint and forget my troubles. It is the best way."

When Gale thought of painting she thought in terms of coloring a picture that was already drawn. But that, apparently, was not what Tassoula meant. She pulled toward her a block of water-color paper on which she had previously sketched a geometrical design, and began to fill it in with bright touches of color. Gale watched her for a while, but in her enormous concentration, Tassoula seemed to forget her cousin's presence, and Gale curled up on the window seat and looked down upon the garden, where Nicos and Warren were walking together. Once they looked up and saw her, and she made the circle with thumb and forefinger she always used with Warren to indicate that everything was all right. He grinned and spoke to Nicos, but the Greek boy did not cheer up as Tassoula had done.

For want of anything else to do, Gale tried a drawing of her own, but it wasn't very successful, and when she discovered that Tassoula had a big folder filled with drawings and paintings she had done, Gale spent the time before dinner looking through them with considerable interest.

Once she broke in upon her cousin's concentration to ask a question. "If you can do work as lovely as this, why do you want to be a dancer?"

Tassoula smeared a bit of green paint absentmindedly on her nose with one finger and considered Gale's words.

"Painting is like breathing for me. But I have no dreams about being a painter as I have about being a dancer. It does not seem very exciting."

"What does your grandfather think of these?" Gale asked, tapping the folder.

"I would never show them to him," Tassoula said quickly. "He would only laugh and make fun of me. He knows too well what good painting is like."

Gale was not so sure that he would laugh, but she could not know him as well as Tassoula did.

The young people had an early dinner, and Nicos said very little during the meal. Tassoula's painting had cheered her, and she and Warren and Gale kept some talk going, comparing Greece and America in one way or another—school and home and friends.

Because of her American mother, Tassoula said, she had a little more freedom than some of her Greek friends. However, sometimes her mother and father disagreed about these matters.

"My father is sometimes very strict and old-fashioned," Tassoula said. "In Greece it is not the custom for girls and boys to play together as you do in America. That is, unless they belong to the same family, as Nicos and I do."

Nicos interrupted, changing the subject abruptly as though he had been lost in his own thoughts and not listening. "Who was that woman who drove you past this house in a car yesterday afternoon?" he asked Warren.

"She's the same one who was in your mother's shop yesterday," Warren told him. "How could you miss that hairdo?"

"I didn't pay much attention to who was in the shop," Nicos said. "But I looked at this woman's face when she was in the car, and the sight of it gave me a strange feeling. As though I must have seen her before sometime. It was not a happy recollection. What is her name?"

"Mrs. Geneva Lambrou," Gale said. "She used to live in Rhodes, so perhaps you knew her then."

"Perhaps," Nicos said. "But I do not recall the name." He shook his head as if to clear his mind of some unpleasant memory and returned to his own obviously gloomy thoughts.

Gale wished she dared ask about the empty wooden box with the Pegasus mark on its side. But she was afraid to. That was a secret between Nicos and Tassoula, and so far neither one had offered to speak about it.

After dinner Warren went off with Nicos, and Gale again accompanied Tassoula to her room. Her cousin returned with such eagerness to her painting that Gale had not the heart to ask her to do something else. Tassoula needed whatever relief from her worries painting might give her, and it was kinder to be patient.

Gale roamed about the room, examining the evzone doll, studying the pictures of Lexine, looking at a few Greek books. They reminded her of Grandfather Thanos' offer of his library if she wanted something to read. This was just the time when a book would help. She told Tassoula what she intended and went into the hall.

Lights had been turned on in the house, and a shaded lamp on a hall table lighted her way toward the closed door of the old man's study. There was no answer to her tap, and she pushed the door open hesitantly. A bar of light from the hall showed her a reading lamp on his desk, and she found her way across the room and switched it on.

At once the study sprang into soft reality, with

bright radiance touching the desk and the terra cotta head of the child Nicos fading into shadow in the far reaches. Along the wide expanse of shelves that made up one wall, book bindings and jackets glowed with color where lamplight touched them, inviting her to dip into their pages. The rhododendrons in the tall Greek jar that stood upon the hearth shone pinky-lavender in the warm light, and there was a scent of some night-blooming flower drifting in through the open window. This was a friendly room that welcomed her and made her feel at home. She had no sense of uneasiness about its shadowy reaches. The unhappy things that had marred its peace in the afternoon had left no troubling mark upon the room. Even the broken bits of clay had been removed from the wastebasket.

Without hesitation, Gale went to an end section and studied some of the English titles. There was a large book about the Dodecanese islands, and she pulled it out to find listed in the contents a section about Rhodes. There were a good many photographs, and this was just the sort of book she would like to borrow. Then, because books always fascinated her, she began to pull other volumes from the shelves, to scan the pages and read a snatch here and there before she put them back.

Near the section of English books was a small ladder that ran smoothly along on wheels to enable the reader to reach the topmost shelves. The ladder was only three steps high and Gale climbed to its top, looking down from this new viewpoint upon the quiet world of Grandfather Thanos' study. The lamplight did not reach so far up here, and the upper shelves were left in shadow.

Idly she pulled out a volume and let the pages fall open. But it was printed in Greek, and she could not read a word. For a few moments she stood on her ladder perch, studying the oddly formed letters, some of which were unlike English letters, though Dad had said that the English alphabet had been taken from that of the ancient Greeks.

After a moment she tried to slip the book back into its slot, but for some reason it would not go in all the say. Some obstruction at the back of the shelf seemed to have slid forward to block the opening. She reached in, her hand small enough to slip easily into the wedge of space. Her fingers touched something hard that she could not identify.

Carefully, she drew out two more books and held them in one arm, while she reached again into the opening. A hard, thin object slipped easily into her fingers, and she drew it out. Even up here in the shadows she could tell at once that it was a square tile with some sort of design painted upon the glazed surface. She tipped it toward the light and saw that a graceful lemon-yellow fish swam across its surface, with a slender stalk of some dark sea vegetation drifting nearby in pale green water.

Excitement began to tingle through her. And curiosity too. The answer to a mystery seemed to be at her very fingertips. With great care she returned the tile to its hiding place, pushing it well back so that it would not block the space when she slipped in the books. Then she drew out other volumes along the shelf, feeling behind each one. All along this shelf, and along the one next to it as well, rows of tiles had been hidden behind rows of books.

When all the volumes were back in place, she came down a step or two on the ladder and sat on its top, her elbows on her knees, her chin in her cupped hands. What else could those tiles be but the ones that belonged to Lexine's gift? Someone had taken them from the wooden box in her room and hidden every one of them behind top-shelf books in Grandfather Thanos' study. Then the box had been carried out to the toolshed and concealed there. But why? What in the world was all this about? Why would anyone choose such a strange hiding place for the tiles?

No answer presented itself to her mind. She knew only that Nicos and Tassoula were together involved in this. But what it meant, she could not guess.

She gave up the puzzle with a regretful sigh because it was tantalizing, and she was curious to know the answer. Then she came down from the ladder, picked up her book about the islands, and moved to the desk to turn off the lamp. At once the room fell into black shadow, with only a bar of light from the hallway reaching a little way into it. For some reason the mood of the room seemed instantly changed. Lamplight had given it soft radiance and a sense of quiet that was right for concentration. The sudden darkness blinded her and whispered of secrets and of something terribly wrong. Now she wanted only to escape the room and the rows of books that offered innocent faces to hide what lay behind. But she took no more than three steps toward the door before her way was blocked.

A shadow loomed against the light as a figure stood in the opening. Recognition was not possible in so brief a glimpse. The person stepped into the room and closed the door very softly behind. She was shut into utter blackness with someone who moved with stealth and who knew his way across the room without hesitation. Yet it was not Grandfather Thanos, who would surely walk with bold assurance into his own study.

Gale found herself close to the big leather chair where the old man had sat. Feeling suddenly frightened, she knelt behind the chair. No matter who had come into the room, she did not want him to know that she was there. The soft and secret movements this intruder made told her clearly that discovery would anger him.

The sounds were scarcely audible as he chose his sure, hushed course across the room. He touched nothing, ran into nothing. He knew his way perfectly. He was very close now. She could feel the faint stir of air caused by his movements. He must have reached the desk, for she heard the click of fingernails on the bronze base of the lamp. Then he found the switch, and the room sprang once more into visible life.

Gale pressed her cheek against the cool leather of the chair back, scarcely daring to breathe. Nearby there was a musical sound that she recognized as the clink of keys on a ring. She heard the secret visitor trying one key after another in a lock. Suddenly one of the keys slid into place with a small metallic sound, and she heard the click of its turning. A drawer was pulled open, and she could hear the fumbling of hands within its depth.

She was more frightened than ever now. If this was some thief, she ought to rouse the house. But if it was a thief and she screamed for help, he might do her harm before anyone could come to her aid. She must force herself to look and see who was there, see what he was doing.

She was already on her knees and she edged toward the place where the chair back made a black line against the light. Very cautiously she peeped out from her kneeling position and saw the identity of the intruder. It was Nicos Castelis who had come so secretly into this room with his grandfather's keys on a ring Gale had once seen in the old man's hands. The light made a bright halo of his blond hair, and his back was toward her. He blocked her sight of the open drawer before which he knelt, but she could tell that he'd found what he wanted. He lifted something out with the greatest care and wrapped it into the folds of a sweater. Then he locked the drawer and reached toward the lamp switch. In relief, Gale sank back to wait for him to leave. And in that instant the floor creaked beneath her knees, and the boy at the desk sprang about in alarm.

8

Dark Mystery

Gale held herself to tensely still that her muscles ached with the strain. Nicos must not find her here. Not when he was doing something that was clearly wrong. This knowledge that had been given her so unexpectedly was something she did not want. She had begun to like and admire Nicos, even while he puzzled her a little. She did not want to know what ugly thing lay behind this secret action of his.

But concealment of her presence was no longer possible. After a long moment of listening, the boy came to the leather chair and pushed it away. Gale knelt on the carpet looking up at him unhappily. His face wore an expression as stern and cold as the look she had seen on his grandfather's face. Strangely, his expression seemed to indicate that Gale Tyler was the guilty one.

"So now you have taken to spying," he snapped. "I must say you look rather foolish crouching there."

His unexpected scorn brought courage and indignation racing back. Gale scrambled to her feet and faced him with her hands on her hips.

"I was here first," she said. "I came to get a book, and I was just going to leave when you sneaked in as though you were a thief."

Nicos cradled the sweater-wrapped object in his arms and blinked as though the word "thief" had struck home. Nevertheless, he attacked again.

"I did not think an American would behave like this," he told her furiously. "You, who talk so much about honor! Honor and—and—" As suddenly as rage had risen in him, it seemed to drain away and he was silent. Gale sensed that he was not so sure of himself as he was pretending to be.

"Honor and what?" she demanded. There was no need to take any more insults from this boy who seemed so anxious to put her in the wrong. "I can tell you something," she flung at him. "I found the place where you hid all those tiles!" She waved one hand toward the bookcases. "Up there on the top shelves. I know all about them!"

For a moment Nicos seemed stunned. Then he collected himself and regarded her more calmly. "What do you intend to do?"

She hadn't really thought about that. "I don't know," she admitted. "I don't know what this is all about, and I don't want to get anyone into trouble when I don't understand what's going on. Especially not Tassoula."

"You are more than kind," he said, and the words carried a bite of mockery.

Gale went on uneasily. "I just hope you're not doing something terribly wrong. Something your grandfather ought to know about."

"That is not for you to judge," the boy said, quite lofty now and superior. "Please remember that it is not I who am a thief."

The keys dangled on their ring between his fingers, and he put them away in a pocket. Then, holding the hidden object against him with one hand, he gestured toward the door with the other. "If you please—after you," he said with elaborate courtesy, as if she had been a grownup.

She tilted her chin haughtily as she went by him, but she said nothing more. He turned off the lamp and came after her at once. At her shoulder he spoke softly.

"It is wiser if you say nothing about these matters. Not now or later."

She did not promise. Once in the hall, she ran away from him and burst into Tassoula's room quite out of breath.

So lost was Tassoula in her painting that she did not even look up, or notice her guest's flustered state. Gale stood beside her cousin, watching over Tassoula's shoulder as she worked, waiting for the thumping of her heart to stop, wondering what to do. What had Nicos meant when he'd said that she must remember it was not he who was a thief? There had been a strange ring of truth in his words, even while he was apparently stealing something from his grandfather's desk. He seemed to be implying that someone else was a thief. Herself, perhaps?

What a horrid boy he was! she thought indignantly. Anyway, she had not promised him to keep quiet about any of this.

"I found the tiles for your sister Lexine's present," she told Tassoula abruptly.

The paint brush in her cousin's fingers slipped and made a crimson smear in the wrong place. She rinsed the brush in water and laid it carefully on a saucer. Then she turned in her chair to look at Gale.

"You—found the tiles?" She sounded as though she did not know where they were hidden.

Gale nodded, puzzled. "Aren't you mixed up in this? Didn't you help Nicos hide the tiles behind the books on the top shelves of your grandfather's study?"

"I did not know the hiding place," Tassoula said softly. "Nicos would not tell me. He said it was better for me not to know what he had done with them. But that is a very good place. Grandfather no longer climbs the ladder. When he wants a book from a high shelf, he calls one of us to get it for him. But those are books he seldom wants these days. They are also safe from too much dusting because he doesn't like the servants to disarrange things in his study. Yes, this was very clever of Nicos."

"Since I know so much," Gale said, "why don't you tell me the rest of the story?"

Tassoula left her painting things and went to the window seat, plumping up the pillow beside her. "Yes, I think it is time to tell you. Come—sit here and we will talk. Turn off the light first, please."

Gale touched the switch and went to sit beside her

cousin in the evening darkness. The soft scent of flowers came to them, sweetly cool on the wind from the sea. Leaves in the garden whispered, and through the wind sounds came the rush and sigh of waves on a stony beach not far away. It was a mingling of sounds that had begun to spell Rhodes and the Aegean to Gale. She leaned her elbows on the window sill and looked up at the bright starlit sky, breathing deeply the garden scents.

"To begin with," Tassoula said, sounding as if it was a relief for her to tell someone, "I had broken a jar that Grandfather valued. I don't know how I ran into it—I just did. He was furious, and he talked as he always does about how I could never be a dancer because I am clumsy. I was afraid he would ask Mother to forbid my practicing at all—even over at the hotel. So I was trying to be very careful and very good.

"I knew about the wonderful present Grandfather had planned for Lexine. She has an apartment in Paris, and she loves to have Greek things about her. So Grandfather designed a tile table especially for her. He seldom works at such things himself any more, but he made for her the most beautiful table top I have ever seen, even painting the tiles himself at the Pegasus, and of course designing it. The tiles made up a scene so imaginative—an underwater dream world of the softest, most delicate colors, with only touches of scarlet and yellow here and there for accent."

Tassoula had been anxious to see the entire table top, she explained. So when she came to the house one evening, Aunt Vera said she might take them out of the wooden box and spread them on the bed in Lexine's room.

"Nicos' mother does not think I am clumsy," Tassoula said. "She tries to encourage me and she does not approve of the way Grandfather opposes my dancing. So she trusted me. And this was a mistake."

In a voice that faltered now and then, Tassoula made Gale see exactly what had happened. With the greatest care her cousin had set all the tiles out on the wide expanse of Lexine's bed. They were numbered on the back so that it was easy to find the right place for each tile to make up the marvelous whole. The scene was dreamily beautiful and soft. Somehow it had reminded Tassoula of dancing. Perhaps Lexine would take inspiration from it and create a dance of her own—a dance of the sea. Tassoula had tried a few steps around Lexine's room, swaying like seaweed, darting like a fish, pretending she was both, pretending she was the sea itself.

Then she had remembered her own gift for her sister and had gone to her room to fetch it. It was a small, heavy bonbon dish she had bought with her own money at Aunt Vera's shop, and she wondered how it would look on the new table top. Feeling light and airy as a dancer, she carried it into Lexine's room to try out the effect. In her hurry, she forgot to be careful. As she ran toward the bed she had tripped, and the small heavy dish had flown out of her hands and crashed down upon the tiles. That the dish had broken did not matter—it was of no great value. But one of the tiles—the one with a scarlet crab on it— had broken into bits, completely ruining the table.

Gale could see her cousin's face, pale in the starlight, with a sheen of tears in her dark eyes.

"I was so frightened," Tassoula said. "I did not dare to tell Aunt Vera. I was terrified of what Grandfather would say when he knew. There was no one but Nicos who could help me. Fortunately, he was home, and I brought him to the room and showed him what I had done. He is kind, Nicos. So good to me, always. And always inventive. He made a plan for me at once. He said we could not risk having Grandfather spread out the tiles and discover that one was missing. Nicos decided he would cause them all to disappear to some safe place for the time being. A place where no one would look, where the servants would not find them in cleaning up. I was to take the broken bits of the crab tile and the dish and hide them—perhaps over at the hotel. Then he would see at once what could be done at the Pegasus to replace the missing tile. Of course he knows all the girls who work there—he spends much time there himself. If something could be arranged, he would signal me with a mirror at nine thirty in the morning in the room where I practice at the hotel. (We had done this before as a sort of game.) But then—things went wrong that morning, and—and—"

"And Warren and I got in the way," Gale finished for her. "To say nothing of Mrs. Lambrou."

"It might still have been all right," Tassoula said sadly, "if only I could have given Nicos the broken pieces of the tile. The design might have been copied and another tile made. But Grandfather has destroyed his pattern the way he chooses to do when he makes an original design that is never to be copied again.

Now only he could make a tile that would truly replace the one that is missing.''

"And it's my fault!" Gale sighed. "Why couldn't I have put those pieces back with the other things? I really didn't mean to carry them to my room in the first place."

"Do not concern yourself," Tassoula said kindly. "I was angry at first. But you are my cousin, and I like you very much. I am not angry any more."

She was glad that Tassoula had forgiven her, but now that she knew the whole story, she could not forgive herself. There ought to be some way in which this unhappy problem could be worked out. Since the trouble was partly her fault, she ought to find a way to mend it.

Tassoula had lost interest in her painting. She began to close her paintbox and dry her brushes.

"Don't put your things away," Gale said. "I think your drawings are awfully good. I don't see why you couldn't design a tile yourself that would take the place of the one that's missing."

Tassoula looked shocked. "How could I match my grandfather's work? Oh, no—I would never dare to try such a thing."

"Why not?" Gale persisted. "I remember the tile very well. I put the pieces together to see what they formed. It wasn't very complicated—just a little red crab swimming around in some sea-green water. I think I have a bit of it that I found on the floor. When I knew I was coming here, I tied it up in a corner of my handkerchief and brought it along."

She untied the knot in her handkerchief to reveal the scrap of tile that showed part of the red crab's claw.

''This gives you the color of the crab and the color of the sea in this part of the design. And it shows where the claw runs off onto the next tile. You could match the exact place.''

Tassoula took the bit of tile and studied it thoughtfully. ''It is very difficult to match colors precisely. Perhaps even Grandfather could not get them twice the very same.''

''Maybe you don't need to be that exact,'' Gale said. ''If you make a really nice tile that matches the general pattern, perhaps it won't matter if it isn't a perfect match. Perhaps your grandfather won't look at it closely enough to notice when he sees the table top again.''

Tassoula shook her head. ''You don't know Grandfather.'' Nevertheless a light had come into her eyes, the light of dawning hope and excitement. Suddenly she bent over her drawing pad and began to sketch lightly with a pencil. She was drawing a crab.

Gale smiled and said nothing more. She got into her pajamas and sat up on her half of Tassoula's huge double bed and turned on the reading lamp on a bedside table. With two hard Greek pillows plumped up behind her, she sat with the book she had brought from Grandfather Thanos' study on her knees, turning the pages.

The photographs were wonderfully large and clear. She found a whole series of pictures of the acropolis of Lindos, with its ruined temple columns standing above steep, rocky cliffs. And she found pictures of Camiros too—the ancient city where the statue group in the museum had been found. In the Camiros pictures there were fewer columns. The place was mostly a great expanse of stone foundations, showing the shape of rooms and doors and streets, all open to be looked into as if a cover had been lifted off. It would be interesting to walk about in such a place.

But even as she studied the pictures and read about the place they represented, the thought of Nicos kept returning at the back of her mind. She had not wanted to tell Tassoula of that scene in the study. The tiles and her finding of them, she was willing to talk about. But she had a curious conviction that Nicos' strange actions, his taking of something from the drawer in his grandfather's desk and hiding it so secretly in his sweater, had nothing at all to do with Tassoula's problem of the broken tile. This was something else, and she had a feeling that it was far more serious and frightening.

The mystery of the broken tile had been answered, only to be replaced by a larger, darker mystery. And this was one she did not want to talk about to Tassoula. Or even to Warren. She wondered what sort of evening her brother was spending with Nicos. What had Warren been doing while Nicos had gone so secretly into his grandfather's study? If Nicos had shown Warren the thing he had taken from the drawer, then perhaps she would have the answer to some of this when she talked to her brother tomorrow.

But for now she was growing sleepy. Even though tomorrow was Monday and a school day for Tassoula, she showed no sign of stopping her work. Apparently she was still sketching crabs and throwing her efforts away, unable to get a design that pleased her. After a few more moments of watching, Gale turned off the bedside lamp and slipped down beneath the covers.

She went to sleep so quickly that she did not know what time Tassoula finally came to bed.

Indeed, when she wakened in the morning, the first thing she saw was her cousin back at the drawing table. If she had not been wearing her school uniform of dark skirt and white blouse, Gale would have thought she had been there all night.

Tassoula smiled, looking cheerful and not at all weary. "What must you think of me?" she said. "You are my guest, yet we have done nothing together. I have not entertained you very well, cousin."

"It doesn't matter," Gale said. "Have you finished your drawing?"

Silently, Tassoula brought her water-color pad to the bed and held out the damp painting for Gale to see. The coloring was dreamy-soft except for the little red crab that swam saucily through the sea. It was a crab with an individuality of its own, and it seemed to reach out with one claw to tweak the tail of a feathery blue fish that was swimming away in alarm.

"What do you think?" Tassoula asked.

"I love it!" Gale said. "It's a wonderful little picture in itself. I should think your grandfather would be proud of you for doing work like this."

Tassoula shook her head, looking as alarmed as the small blue fish. "It must not stand out as something in itself. This afternoon, when we go to the Pegasus, I will try to use this design in painting a tile. I have often painted at the factory for my own amusement."

"Shouldn't you spread out the other tiles so you can check your drawing with them?"

"How can I? It would be too dangerous. I would not be able to match it exactly in any case, and I do not want to risk being discovered. There is no time to waste.''

''Never mind,'' Gale said. ''If you've replaced the tile, the result can't be as awful as if your grandfather found a gap in his pattern. Once the tile is made, perhaps you could show it to your grandfather and tell him the whole story.''

''I could never do that!'' Tassoula insisted. ''You do not know how stern and frightening he can be. I cannot bear it if he is angry with me again. Do hurry and get up, please. Then we can have breakfast together before I leave for school.''

Gale hurried, and when they went downstairs to the dining room they found that Nicos had left for school with a friend, and Aunt Marjorie had come to take Tassoula to her girls' school. Warren was eating slowly and dreamily, not much interested in the talk around him.

Tassoula seemed disappointed to find Nicos gone. Probably she had hoped to show him her drawing and ask for his advice, Gale thought. Now that would have to wait until late in the afternoon when they all met again at the Pegasus.

When Tassoula and her mother had gone, Warren and Gale walked back to the hotel and Gale told her mother the story of the tiles and of the predicament Tassoula was in. Mother was sympathetic and hoped things would turn out all right. She offered no advice, and Gale knew she would not talk to her sister about Tassoula's secret. Nevertheless, Gale could not bring herself to mention Nicos and his odd behavior last night. Warren seemed to have noticed nothing strange about the actions of the Greek boy. He said that Nicos had gone off on some errand once during the evening, but otherwise they had been together. Evidently Nicos had offered his guest no confidences as to what he had been doing.

When they reached the hotel, Mother suggested a morning's drive through some of the small villages outside of Rhodes. Uncle Alexandros lent them his car, and Mother had a driving permit, so this was a pleasant way to spend the morning. Following the map, they took the well-paved road to Mount Philerimos. At the top of the mountain there was a medieval monastery and the few ruins that remained of Ialysos, one of the three ancient cities of Rhodes. From the brow of the mountain there was a marvelous view of this end of the island, clear into the town of Rhodes.

They stood in a high, windy place where a wide stone platform had been built, and looked all about— from the sea and the coastline to the mountains of Rhodes rising in the interior.

It was here that Mother made her astonishing announcement. "You remember that odd little woman in the wig at the hotel—Mrs. Lambrou? She has rented a car, you know, and this morning at breakfast she invited me to bring you on a drive to Camiros with her one day later this week."

"Oh, no!" Warren said, making a face.

Gale said nothing. She was not really surprised by this new move, just increasingly uneasy.

"I thought you'd enjoy the trip!" Mother said, disappointed at Warren's exclamation and Gale's silence.

"Camiros is a place I especially want to see," Warren admitted. "But not with Mrs. Lambrou."

Mother shook her head, mildly disapproving.

"You're being unkind. She seems to have gone out of her way to invite us. Perhaps she's lonely for American company, even though she is Greek. You mustn't let that exaggerated wig and the blue stuff she puts on her eyes prejudice you. She's very young. I think she'll outgrow that sort of thing, given time."

A word came into Gale's mind. A very good word for Geneva Lambrou. One that she had read in a story before she left home.

"I think she's a malevolent person," she said.

"Mal—which?" asked Warren.

Mother raised her eyebrows. "That's a very strong word to use. Are you sure you know what it means?"

"I looked it up at home," Gale said. "It means 'wishing evil,' 'disposed to injure,' 'having a baleful influence.' "

"And what does 'baleful' mean?" Warren caught her up at once.

Feeling pleased because she had looked that word up too, Gale went on sounding like a dictionary. " 'Baleful' means 'full of deadly, or pernicious, influence.' But don't ask me what 'pernicious' means. I had to stop somewhere."

Mother seemed to have had her breath blown away by the wind. "Well! I must say—" she gasped. Then she turned to Gale quite seriously and laid a hand against her cheek. "I'm glad you looked up the words so you know what they mean. But I don't think you should use such words with so little reason. I doubt that this unfortunate little woman is disposed to injure anyone. And to say that she intends evil is certainly going too far. I would hate to see a daughter of mine adopt a prejudiced attitude toward someone she doesn't really know. It's likely that if we can get Mrs. Lambrou out from under that wig, she'll be quite likable.''

"I've seen her without the wig," Warren said. "And I didn't like her then either. But I guess all that about baleful influence is pretty strong.''

Thus outvoted, Gale said nothing more. Mother was always sunny-tempered, kindhearted, and ready to trust and like everyone. This was a good way to be, of course. But Mother had not seen Geneva Lambrou as her son and daughter—and especially her daughter—had seen her. Gale still felt that malevolent was a good word, and she did not look forward to a trip as the guest of Mrs. Lambrou. There was something very wrong there, and when it came out someone might very well be injured.

9

Nicos'
Astonishing Plan

Just before the time when school closed for the day, Aunt Marjorie drove Mother, Warren, and Gale across town to the place where Pegasus pottery was made. On the way they stopped at Tassoula's school and picked her up. Tassoula dropped her schoolbooks into the back of the car, but kept a Manila envelope in her hands. It was her painting for the tile design, Gale knew.

The pottery plant was on a hillside above and behind the old city. Aunt Marjorie drove the car into an open space where other cars were parked. They got out and walked toward the unpretentious, low-lying building, with Tassoula eagerly leading the way. Nicos came to the door to welcome them.

Gale watched him warily. This was the first time she had seen him since the unfortunate encounter in his grandfather's study, and she was not sure how he would behave toward her. She found out quickly enough. While he was friendly toward Warren and Mother, he treated Gale with a formal courtesy that hid his real feelings. It was evident that he did not trust her and that he had not forgiven her for what had happened last night. The knowledge made her tongue-tied, so that she could find nothing to say to him.

Since several customers were waiting for the plant manager in the showroom, he put the task of showing the guests around into Nicos' willing hands. Nicos made an excellent guide because of his interest in all that had to do with the making of Pegasus pottery. Watching him with an attention she tried to conceal, Gale soon realized that he knew all about the workings of the plant.

He led them first to a damp-smelling room where skilled workmen sat at pottery wheels, shaping rough clay into jars and vases with amazing speed. One of them good-naturedly let Warren try his hand at the wheel, and he found it much more difficult than it looked to shape the spinning clay into the proper form.

They saw the kilns where the shapes were baked at tremendous heat, and then went into the big bright room filled with long tables at which young girls sat working. Here glazes and decorations were brushed on, and intricate designs were painted by the quick, skilled fingers of the girls. While Mother, Warren, and Aunt Marjorie were occupied watching at one of the tables, Tassoula touched Nicos on the arm and drew him quietly aside. She nodded to Gale to come too, and the three went to stand beside a window where bright, clear light poured into the room. Tassoula took her water color from the envelope and held it out to Nicos. She did not explain, but waited for him to comment.

He knew what it was intended for and whistled softly under his breath.

"It is a good attempt," he said. "It is amazingly good work in itself, cousin. But I do not think it will fit the pattern of the other tiles."

"It is the only thing I can think of to do," Tassoula told him. "Will you let me try, please? I mean, putting it on a tile."

When Nicos smiled, his sea-green eyes lighted up and he looked like a different boy, Gale thought—friendly and not at all frightening.

"You shall try, cousin," he said. "One of the girls is out today. You may have her place at the table over there."

His smile did not include Gale, and he paid no attention to her as he led Tassoula to the table and explained in Greek to the other girls that she wanted to try a design of her own on a tile. Gale watched for a little while as Nicos helped Tassoula in her choice of colors and gave her some advice. When he returned to Mother and Aunt Marjorie, Gale followed, wishing he would not act as though she did not exist. As though she had done something wrong and was beneath his notice!

"What is Tassoula up to?" Aunt Marjorie inquired.

"It is a secret," Nicos said quickly. "She wishes to work alone at something for a surprise."

They continued their inspection of the room, pausing to look at vases and tiles and pottery jars that the girls were decorating in one way and another. The designs seemed to be established, and each girl worked from a pattern she knew well, performing her individual task with the quick skill of much practice.

Beyond the big workroom was the showroom—a fascinating place with shelves along the walls and a long show table down the middle. Every inch of space was heaped with fine Pegasus pottery, and Mother decided at once that she must have some of these things to send home as gifts.

Warren, who had been fascinated by this work with clay, seemed equally interested in the final designs and shapes.

"Some of these look exactly like pieces we saw in the museum," he told Nicos.

The Greek boy shook his head. "Not exactly. It is impossible that they should be. But we try to preserve many of the old designs. They are very popular with tourists who buy in the shops." He took down a tall jar with two handles at the neck and showed it to Warren. "This is an amphora made in an ancient pattern. It was used for storing wine or other liquids."

The jar was iron-red in color, with black figures in silhouette around its plump sides. Below the human figures ran a Grecian key, with further abstract designs narrowing into the base.

"Tassoula says old things are still being discovered," Warren remarked.

"Of course," said Nicos. "So much has been lost that there must be many treasures still waiting to be unearthed. All over Greece the search goes on. We are all treasure hunters, in a sense."

"It would be pretty exciting to find something," Warren sounded dreamy again. "Even something small and unimportant—if it was really ancient."

"There have been important finds in our century," Nicos reminded him. "The statue of the famous Charioteer at Delphi, and the young Venus of Rhodes, found by chance in our own waters. To say nothing of the marvelous discoveries of Heinrich Schliemann less than a hundred years ago."

"I've read a lot about Schliemann," Warren said eagerly.

"You haven't mentioned your grandfather's discovery of that statue group at the museum," Gale put in.

Once more Nicos seemed to shy away from mention of that particular marble. Perhaps he did not want to seem proud of anything his grandfather had done, what with this antagonism existing between them. He was a strange boy, this Nicos Castelis.

"I have been at Mycenae," he told Warren. "I have seen what Schliemann found."

The note of excitement grew in Warren's voice. "When we were in Athens I saw the golden mask that Schliemann discovered at Mycenae. He thought it was the death mask of King Agamemnon."

Gale remembered the astonishingly beautiful mask made from a flat sheet of gold with the unforgettable features pressed into it. She remembered that Warren had stood so raptly before the mask that it had been difficult to draw him away.

"You have great interest in the past," Nicos said, regarding Warren with a wondering look, as if he found it surprising that an American should feel this way.

"Of course I have," Warren agreed. "Dad says the past of Greece is *us*—much more than we sometimes remember. Because of all the fine things ancient Greece gave to Western civilization, it's important to know all we can about it."

"If you feel this way, you must keep your eyes open in Rhodes," Nicos said. "Strange things have happened here. Even in places where supposedly thorough excavation has been done, objects have been found."

This was going a little far, it seemed to Gale. It wasn't likely that Warren would stumble onto some important find during their stay on the island, and she wished that Nicos wouldn't raise her brother's hopes unduly. With such encouragement, he'd start looking under every stone, and it would waste more time than picture-taking.

When Mother had selected the pieces she wanted to send home and a girl had written down the details of shipping them, the visitors were ready to leave. Aunt Marjorie offered to drop Nicos off at his home on her way back to the hotel, and asked him to see if Tassoula was ready to come with them.

Nicos returned with word that Tassoula was still working. She did not want to show anyone what she had done yet, nor did she want to stop. Nicos said he would stay and they would come home together when the Pegasus closed for the day.

Aunt Marjorie agreed and drove the others back to the hotel.

A half hour or so before dinner, Gale came down from her room. The sun had not yet set, and the sky over the sea was splendidly beautiful in shades of gold and rose and aquamarine. She told Mother she would go for a walk and went out to explore one of the curving streets near the hotel.

There was a place she had noticed several times as they had passed it, and Mrs. Lambrou had pointed it out from the car as an old Turkish cemetery. Its iron gateway stood open, and a grassy expanse spread beneath widely spaced eucalyptus trees. Gale had seen such trees on a visit to California and knew them by their ragged bark and long, thin, leathery leaves. The marble stones of the cemetery were grouped in a tight cluster in one place and contained within a low wall. The stones tipped and leaned, and some of the marble turbans that topped them were askew. The place was like a pleasant park, and Gale wandered toward the stones, moving idly.

On the far side of the park stood a small mosque, and a man in Moslem dress came to its door and stared at her. She hesitated, uncertain that she was welcome in this place, but when he saw her pause, he smiled and spoke. His words were in a foreign tongue—Turkish, probably—but she understood his gesture of welcome. He did not mind if she walked here.

At this sunset hour the wind had hushed as if about to make a change. The eucalyptus leaves hung limp overhead, and the only sound that reached her through the quiet was the rush and retreat of waves on nearby beaches.

She forgot about time and sat down on the grass cross-legged, with the shadows long about her. She began to dream a little, letting pleasant thoughts drift through her mind. How long she sat there in the sunset peace, she did not know. It was the sound of footsteps on dry leaves scattered across the grass that made her look around.

Nicos was coming toward her through the grove.

"They said you had come in this direction, and I saw you from the street," he told her. "Before I brought Tassoula to the hotel, we stopped at my house, and I have something for you that my mother said you forgot to take, though you had asked to borrow it."

He held out the book about the Dodecanese islands that she had been looking at in Tassoula's room last night. Pleased that he should be so unexpectedly considerate, but puzzled too, she stood up and took the book. Why had he brought it to her instead of leaving it with Tassoula at the hotel?

He seemed in no hurry to go. For once he did not look so disapproving of her as he had since their meeting in his grandfather's study. She had the feeling that he was struggling with himself in some way—as though he wanted to say something to her, but did not know how to begin.

"Have you stopped being angry with me?" she asked directly.

He looked a little embarrassed. "Perhaps I should not have been angry with you at all. But I was not certain that you wouldn't tell anyone about my being in Grandfather's study last night. I am glad you have kept silent."

"I didn't want to tell anyone," Gale said. "I didn't know what your being there meant, and it was really none of my business."

He seemed to lose himself in deep thought, staring

for a long moment at the tipsily leaning gravestones with their tilted turbans. The quick darkness of the Mediterranean thickened around them, and the wind sighed in the trees overhead, stirring the leaves to life. Gale felt the cool touch of evening upon her cheeks and turned toward the gate.

"Shall we go back?" she said.

"No—wait!" Nicos put out a hand to stop her. "There is something I would like to do for your brother Warren. He tells me you are going to visit Camiros later this week. Would it not be fine if he could find something there? Something old and valuable?"

Gale stared at him in astonishment. She could no longer see his face clearly in the shadow of the trees, and it was hard to tell whether or not he was joking.

"Are you teasing me?" she asked uncertainly.

"No—no, of course not." Nicos sounded impatient again. "If Warren will search in the right place, it may be that he will find the sort of treasure he wishes to unearth."

None of this made sense to Gale. How could Nicos know where treasure would be found? If he knew, he would not leave it there. He would unearth it himself.

"I don't know what you're talking about," she said.

"Look!" He took the book from her hands and flipped it open to a place where a marker had been inserted between the pages. "There is a picture here of Camiros—very clear and in much detail. You cannot see it now. It is too dark. But if you will study it when you go to the hotel, you will see that I have placed a small pencil mark in one particular place. On the day when you go to Camiros you will remind your brother of what I told him today—that objects are still found on occasion in Greece. Undoubtedly, he will begin to search a little as he walks among the ruins. You will pretend to help him and you will find a way to lead him in a particular direction. Perhaps you will begin to dig a little yourself in this place that I have marked. You will call to Warren to help you, and he will come to take the stick from your hands. You will thus be sure that he digs in the right place. Do you understand what I mean?''

She did not understand at all and she did not like any of this. ''I don't want to fool Warren and play an unkind trick on him,'' she told Nicos heatedly. ''There would be nothing to find.''

''If you do your part, there will be something to find,'' Nicos assured her.

''But it wouldn't be real! I don't want to fool him like that.'' She would have turned away from this strange, intense boy, but Nicos put his hands on her shoulders and held her where she was.

''Listen to me, please,'' he said. ''There will be a treasure to find and it will be real. It will give your brother great pride and satisfaction to discover it. You must urge that he take it at once to the museum and put it in the hands of the authorities. They will be grateful to him, and he will be famous all over Greece as a young American who found what everyone else had missed.''

He had not convinced her at all. This was some sort of trick, and she would have nothing to do with it. She wriggled her shoulders out of his grasp and ran toward the iron gate, leaving the book in his hands.

Nicos hurried after her in angry exasperation. "You Americans are as pigheaded as—as any Greek!" he shouted.

"All right!" said Gale over her shoulder. "So I'm pigheaded. I won't do something that is cheating and dishonest. I won't fool Warren like that."

Nicos came with her and when they reached the sidewalk, where streetlights shone upon them, she glanced at him and saw that all the anger had gone out of him. He looked tragic now, and despairing, as if he had suffered some terrible defeat.

"A Greek has honor too," he said. "The equal of any American."

"Why don't you tell me why you want to do a thing like this?" Gale asked. "I don't think it's just to give Warren a thrill."

"You are right," he agreed. "It is not. But the secret is not mine to tell. I can say only that in this way you may save the Castelis name from great disgrace and my grandfather from much suffering. It is not a wrong thing to do. It is a good thing, and if you will help me, perhaps a very old mistake may be corrected."

As he spoke in this earnest, almost tragic way, her resolution began to waver. "But why Warren? Why must you do this through him?"

"Because it is a natural thing," Nicos explained, his eagerness returning as he sensed that she had weakened. "Your brother has this strong interest, this desire to learn about archaeology, to find something himself. He is honest and he will be innocent of any knowledge that he has been led to this place. I have thought of no other way that might not cause suspicion to fall upon the Castelis name. The authorities will have only a young visitor from America to deal with. They will be convinced. No Castelis will be in the vicinity of the find. If I am there, I will not be seen. Tassoula will be in school. You will make the trip with your mother and brother and the Lambrou woman who wears a wig. All will be innocent.''

"*I* won't be so innocent," Gale objected.

"You *must* be," Nicos said. "In reality, you know nothing. There is nothing I have told you that gives you the answer. You will need to keep silent only about what I have asked you to do. That is all. If you will do this small, harmless thing, you will save my grandfather from suffering and grief.''

They had nearly reached the hotel. A band of light from the lobby lay across the flagged terrace in front. In her mind Gale could see the face of Grandfather Thanos with those grooves of sadness marking his cheeks. Grandfather Thanos, who had been kind to a young American stranger, who had lost his son in the war, and was disappointed in his grandson Nicos.

"You have begun to love him too," Nicos said softly. "This is true, is it not?"

She looked up into the face of the tall, fair-haired boy beside her. Light fell upon it, and she saw in his pale green eyes a look she had never seen there before. An unguarded look of love for his grandfather, of soft pleading, of a longing to undo some wrong. Her last defense went down.

"Give me the book," she said. "I'll do my best if you can promise that it's nothing wrong or harmful. And when we get home to the States I'll tell Warren the truth. Though I'm afraid it will hurt him then, if he is very pleased with his find.''

''Thank you,'' Nicos said and handed her the book. ''On my honor as a Greek I can promise this.'' He did not seem to think that Warren's hurt feelings mattered, for he did not comment on that at all.

He left her at the hotel steps, and she stood watching his tall, slim figure stride off down the street. Then she mounted the steps with the book in her hands, its marker still in place.

10

Hidden Treasure

After dinner that night Gale went to her room and sat with the book about the islands in her lap. She opened it to the place where a slip of paper lay between the pages and stared at the large, clear photograph.

The picture had been taken from below on a gently sloping hillside. Running solidly up the hill and covering every inch of space, lay the foundations of what had once been the ancient Greek city of Camiros. As she had noted before, the foundations lay open, and all was level and could be seen clearly. Only on the ridge of hill at the very top were six graceful columns rising above the rest. Down through the center of the town and across its width ran aisles that must be streets.

At first she could not see the mark Nicos had mentioned. Not until she tilted the photograph toward the

light did the shine of a small "X" in pencil catch her
eye. In this place stone walls came together at an
angle, and beyond the walls and above, grassy earth
rose toward another ridge. Near the base of a gnarled
pine tree on the hillside Nicos had placed the mark.
Here, clearly, the excavating of the town had stopped.
Perhaps because there seemed nothing more to excavate. But it might, just possibly, be a place where
no one had tried to dig. She only hoped she could
bring Warren to this place and get him to search.
Sometimes he had strong ideas of his own and paid
no attention to her suggestions. Anyway, the whole
thing seemed quite uncertain, and she still did not
like it.

Gale sat for a while with the book on her knees,
wondering about Nicos and his strange plan. She
could bring herself to do as he asked only because of
Grandfather Thanos. It was true that an affection for
the old man had sprung up in her almost at once.
From her first meeting with him in the garden, she
had liked him and had felt in response his own liking
for her. There had been no doubt about Nicos' sin-
cerity when he said this plan was being done only for
Grandfather Thanos' sake. In spite of the antagonism
that seemed to exist between the boy and his grandfather, Gale could not help believing that love for the
old man lay beneath the surface of Nicos' outward
resentment.

The next few days passed quickly enough. Too
quickly, in some ways, because Gale had begun to
dread the coming trip. One bright spot had been a
phone call from Dad. Things were going well in Ath-

ens, he said, and he hoped to join them in Rhodes for a weekend visit a week from next Saturday.

On Friday morning the group of four started for Camiros right after breakfast. Mother sat in front beside Geneva Lambrou while Warren and Gale sat in the back seat of the car.

Gale found herself edgy and worried—almost the way she felt at school right before an examination. Last night, and again this morning, she had studied the photograph, trying to memorize landmarks in order to make sure of the place. But now that they were on the way, she began to feel that she had forgotten the entire plan of the town and would not be able to fit any of it to that photograph.

The road they took out of Rhodes ran beside the sea, with small villages along the way. There were many of the cloth-winged windmills of the island, turning in the breeze. Now and then they passed women riding sideways on donkeys, with their booted feet dangling toward the ground as the small animals jogged along with their burdens. Often the women had covered their heads and half their faces with scarves, which gave them a veiled, oriental look. But Geneva said it was only to protect them from the sun.

Since she had lived in Rhodes as a young girl, Geneva knew the way. She made the turn where the road ran away from the sea and through woods toward the interior of the island. Mother was very friendly and kind, and Geneva seemed to be responding, Gale thought—as everyone did to Mother.

In the back seat, Warren was quiet, lost in one of his absent moods, and Gale was content to concentrate on her own concerns. Not until she heard Geneva's voice rising in a new complaint and caught the name of Thanos Castelis, did she pay attention and begin to listen.

"You can imagine how I felt!" Geneva exclaimed. "I was very courteous in my approach, but he did not so much as invite me into the garden. The yard boy who saw me at the gate took me to the old man where he was sitting on a bench, and I told him what I wished most pleasantly."

"To take photographs of his house and garden, you mean?" Mother asked.

Geneva took her eyes from the road to look at Mother in a way that made Gale nervous about the car. "Yes, of course. I was most flattering and complimentary. But he looked at me as if I were a worm, and said *no*. Just like that! He was very rude and cold. He did not invite me inside at all, though I hinted that I would like to see his famous house. He said it was not famous and it was not open to the public. Never will I forgive him—never! It is one more count against him."

"It does seem a little strange," Mother said gently. "The Greeks are usually very hospitable people."

Gale did not find it altogether strange. She suspected that Geneva Lambrou had not been so courteous as she imagined. It was more likely that she had been demanding, so that she had offended the old man and he'd wanted nothing to do with her. Besides, with that huge wig and her blue-smudged eyes, she was scary in daylight. Gale was sure that Grandfather Thanos would not have approved of her and thus had been less hospitable than usual.

"The time will come when I will show him who I

am and what I can do," Geneva ran on. "Who does he think he is—that old man—to treat me in such a manner?"

"Did you bring your camera with you today?" Warren asked suddenly. "I brought mine."

Geneva shook her head impatiently. "No—it is only houses that I wish to take pictures of."

Once more Gale wondered if the picture-taking was just an excuse Geneva used in her efforts to get into Grandfather Thanos' house for some secret reason of her own. Though why she should wish this if she regarded him as an enemy was hard to guess.

Geneva was grumbling again. "I will find a way. I have an old score to settle with that one." She glanced at Mother again. "Perhaps you will intercede for me, so that I may get my pictures?"

"When you feel the way you do about him?" Mother asked in surprise. She might be friendly and generous most of the time, but she did not lack the backbone to stand up for what she thought was right when it seemed necessary. She went on with a faint note of disapproval in her voice. "You must remember that we are related to Mr. Castelis by marriage. I really don't think you should speak of him in such a manner, Mrs. Lambrou."

Geneva threw her a startled look, but she made no apology. She merely shrugged as though it did not matter and said nothing more until they turned off the road into a cleared space in the woods where she parked the car.

"We have arrived," she said shortly.

Gale got out of the car with the others and stood looking around. If this was Camiros, it did not look like the pictures. There were a few excavations below the path where they stood, but nothing that resembled the photographs she had seen. A man wearing the cap of an official was coming toward them. Geneva spoke to him in Greek and then turned to Mother.

"I tell him we do not wish a guide," she said. "Come with me—I know the way very well."

They followed a dirt path around the excavated section and up a little ridge of hill where pine trees grew. As they topped the ridge they were suddenly in the open and the ancient city lay spread in full view at their very feet. It was breathtaking to come upon it so unexpectedly. The empty stone rooms ran in a solid mass from the six slim columns at the top, downhill toward the incredibly blue Aegean sea that Camiros never reached. At the lower end were a few broken pillars and the open space of some sort of hall or market. Below was a drop-off into space, and beyond that in the distance where the coastline lay, was the sea. The two sides of the town were marked by ridges of hill.

Gale stole a look at her brother and saw that he was lost in his own dream. This place was more ancient than anything else they had seen, and she knew he was caught by its spell. He went ahead down the dirt path and into the very heart of the ruins, taking his camera out of its case, not waiting for the others. Gale watched him go, feeling a little guilty because of what she was about to do, because of the hoax she must play upon him.

The two women followed, picking their way more slowly. Gale stayed where she was for a few moments, trying to study the plan of the town in order to see it as the photograph had shown it to her. But now she stood at a different viewpoint from that which the photographer had chosen, and nothing except those columns at the top seemed recognizable.

As she looked toward them anxiously, she caught a flicker of movement in their shadow. She had no more than a glimpse of the boy who stood there, tall and straight and fair-haired. Then he was gone, and she knew he had moved behind a column and out of sight. It was Nicos, of course. He had hinted that he might be here, but he would not want the others to see him. His presence gave her both comfort and an increasing sense of worry. Perhaps he would help her if she failed in her purpose. On the other hand, his presence gave her no chance for retreat. She must go ahead, no matter what happened.

Drawing a deep breath, she went down the path onto the wide paved street that cut across the town. Now that she was in the midst of the ruins, she saw that the walls came hardly to her waist in height and spread out in all directions. The entire expanse of stone was a dusty wheat-color in the warm light that spilled out of the sky. Overhead a few popcorn clouds were blown along through vivid blue air. It was a beautiful scene—but empty of all life, and utterly still.

Or it would have been still had it not been for the chattering of Geneva Lambrou. It was as if the little woman had need to remind herself that she was alive when everything about her was so still in this long-dead city. It was a relief when Mother put a quiet hand on her arm, stilling her chatter.

"Hush," she said. "Let Camiros sleep. We mustn't waken it."

Once more, Geneva looked startled, but she hushed for a few moments, and when Mother started up the wide main avenue toward the temple at the top, Geneva followed her. Gale hoped that Nicos would slip out of their path in time.

Warren had taken the avenue that led toward the lower part of the town, and Gale turned in the same direction. He had stepped into one of the small rooms and was already taking pictures. When she came near, he looked at her raptly.

"Can you see it the way it must have been—perhaps twenty-five hundred years ago?" he said softly. "Long before the birth of Christ there were people living in these houses. The walls were high and there were roofs, and the temple to the gods stood up there on the hill where there are only six columns left. And there were statues everywhere. Look—look here!"

He bent above a block of the cream-tinted Rhodes stone and pointed to an indentation. It looked as though the footprint of a man had been set into the stone.

"A statue stood there once," Warren said. "Perhaps one of those statues we saw in the museum in Rhodes. They often made places like footprints in the stone for the statues to stand."

Gale glanced toward her mother and Geneva, who were climbing the bank toward the temple columns. The sun threw shadows across the stone, but nothing stirred up there and there was no sound except the singing of birds and the rush of wind in the pine trees that rimmed two sides of the town.

She did not look at Warren as she made the first move in the game. "Perhaps this would be a good place to search for something old. Wouldn't it be fun to find even scraps of a vase or dish, if it were really ancient?"

"I thought of that before we got here," Warren said. "But you can see the place has been picked clean. All its bones are showing. Every one of these little rooms has been cleaned out carefully. I'm sure every ounce of earth has been sifted, so nothing of value would be missed. That's the way it's done, you know."

Gale waved a hand toward the far side of the town—the side where Nicos had placed the mark on the photograph.

"Just the same, they had to stop digging somewhere," she pointed out. "No one has excavated up there. Who knows what the earth might hide?"

Warren shook his head. "They probably stopped because that's as far as the town went. Besides, anything that was buried up there would probably lie under tons of earth."

"We could try," Gale said. "I thought you wanted to."

He grinned at her. "I didn't know you were so interested in archaeology. What would we dig with? Our hands?"

"Oh, you!" cried Gale impatiently. "You talk about finding treasures all the time, and then when you have a chance, you won't even try."

"It's enough to be here," Warren said. "You go and dig if you want to. I'd just like to walk around the town and think about the way it used to be. And get some pictures."

He moved downhill toward the open marketplace

where a few broken columns stood, and left Gale to do as she pleased. She could see that he wasn't going to be cooperative, and she didn't know whether she was glad or sorry.

Still uncertain of the plan of the real town as it compared to the picture, she wandered toward the far edge and stood looking up at the pine grove above. In the hot sun the scent of pine was so heavy on the air that it was almost something she could taste. She sat upon a low wall and looked about her thoughtfully. A small, brown lizard came out of a crevice and gazed at her with bright, curious eyes. She sat very still so as not to frighten it and watched the puffing in and out of breath in the pouch at its throat. How tiny and perfectly formed he was! A small prehistoric monster that was the only thing that now belonged to this lonely place.

From among the pine trees came a faint whistle. It trilled insistently, then was silent. Gale knew it was meant for her ears alone. She climbed onto a wall and stood up to scan the woods. In a flash the lizard vanished. Gale searched the ridge of the hill with a slow, careful gaze.

Something moved among dark pine trunks, and for an instant Nicos was again in view. He flung something toward her and pointed. A small sturdy tree branch came flying through the air to fall just above her on the hillside. Gale threw a hasty look at Warren, but he was lost in his own exploration and paying no attention to his sister. When she looked toward the pine trees again, Nicos was out of sight. But she knew he was watching, and she had received her instructions clearly.

It was not difficult to scramble up the hillside from the level of the wall. Earth slid a little beneath her feet, and the white tops of Queen Anne's lace brushed against her as she climbed. A bush here gave her a hand hold, and a tree trunk there. She picked up the stick Nicos had thrown and looked in the direction in which he had pointed.

Now, quite suddenly, she could see the pattern as she had seen it in the picture. Everything fell into recognizable place. There was the right angle where the walls met, with a gnarled pine tree growing above. It was at the foot of such a tree that Nicos had placed his pencil mark. She began to feel excited now. Excited and eager. The whole thing had begun to seem real and not at all like a hoax. She did not know what would be found up there, but she had a feeling that it would be something more than a mere shard of broken pottery.

When she reached the foot of the tree, it was easy to see that the ground had recently been disturbed in this place. Someone had made a slight effort to restore the carpet of pine needles, but the earth beneath was loose and crumbly. It did not matter. By the time Gale had dug into it for a while, no one would know of the earlier disturbance. She knelt on the soft pine carpet and began to poke into the loose earth with her stick.

Almost at once the wood seemed to strike something hard buried in the ground. She stood up and shouted for Warren.

"Come and help me!" she called. "I'm not very good at digging, but I think I've found something up here."

For a moment she thought he would not come. He had turned from his contemplation and was clearly laughing at her.

"Please come," she urged. "Warren, I think there really is something here."

He came slowly, taking his own good time. Once he stopped to take a shot of Camiros from a new angle, and he did not hurry climbing the bank. When at last he stood beside her, she showed him that her stick had struck something when she prodded it into the earth. He was not impressed.

"I expect it's just another rock," he said. "The hillside is full of them. But if you want it for a souvenir, I'll dig it out for you."

He took the stick from her hand and began to dig a circle around the object in the earth. In nearby treetops the very birds were still, as if they held their breath and watched. Only the wind that had blown across Camiros for thousands of years refused to hush, and a salty breath from the sea laced through the scent of pine.

Warren slid one end of the stick into the circle he had dug and began to pry gently beneath the hard central object. As he pried around the circle, the reddish earth began to crack and fall away, and suddenly something creamy white was visible in the pit.

"There is something here," Warren said, his tone suddenly quiet. "I don't think it's just a rock."

He threw the stick aside and began to dig into the earth with both hands, seeking to grasp the buried object. Gale's heartbeats thudded in her ears, and she could almost feel the eyes of Nicos Castelis watching them.

The object Warren was lifting from the earth was clearly made of marble. The last crumbs of earth and dry pine needles fell away, and Warren knelt, holding the object up reverently for her to see.

The thing he had unearthed was a graceful marble hand. The fingers were extended, curled only a little, as though the hand reached out in pleading. It was a young woman's hand, softly rounded, its back faintly dimpled, the mounds of the palm full-fleshed in the creamy marble. The break from the original arm came just above the wrist, jagged where the marble had cracked through, the vein of the stone visible. It was not meant to be a hand by itself. It was part of a whole. Somehow it had a strangely beseeching look in its helpless, reaching beauty, as if it asked something of them, begged them for help.

Warren had been struck speechless. He held the marble hand, staring at it in astonished delight. Even Gale was caught by the spell of this enchantment. In her excitement, she forgot Nicos, forgot the hoax of which she was a part.

"It must have broken off from a statue!" she cried. "Warren, maybe the rest of it is buried here. Do you think we could dig some more and—"

"Take it easy," he said, though not unkindly. "Don't chatter like a monkey. I want to think."

Gale picked up the stick and began to make aimless forays into the earth around her until Warren reached out to take it from her hands.

"Stop it! If there's a whole statue buried here, we aren't going to dig it up with a branch from a tree. The first thing to do is mark the place where we found this. Then we can bring the proper people back and show them the spot if we need to.''

He took a rather grimy handkerchief from his pocket and wrapped the marble hand carefully in it. Then he began to pick up chunks of rock and set them into the earth around the hole, pounding one rock into the ground with the weight of another, so they could not be easily dislodged. From among the trees a whistle trilled again. Abruptly Gale came to her senses. That was Nicos, and there wasn't any statue. This hand might be an archaeological treasure, but it had been put here very recently by Nicos Castelis.

''If it's really something old, you'd better take it to the museum right away,'' she said, remembering the rest of Nicos' instructions. ''We ought to get it back to town and—''

''I know what to do with it,'' Warren said, sounding disgruntled. ''Do stop squealing and jumping around. Of all the beginner's luck! Here I wouldn't even look, and you come right up the hill and pick out the one place where something is buried that everyone else has missed.''

She was glad he had turned back to the business of finishing his circle of stones and thus did not see the bright red flush that swept into her face, warming her to the very roots of her hair.

''It was your find,'' she said quickly. ''I—I wasn't strong enough to dig it out. I didn't know how.''

''I don't really mind,'' he said. ''The big thing is that we've really found something.''

''Do you think it's something important?''

''I don't know for sure,'' Warren said. ''It could

be. Why would anything that wasn't very old be buried in a place like this?''

Gale stared around toward the woods, frowning a little. Nothing of Nicos could be seen. He would be satisfied now that she had done what she was supposed to do, and she could only hope that it would serve Grandfather Thanos well, as Nicos had claimed it would.

Warren finished his task of marking the place and picked up the hand again. Now a reaction to what had happened seemed to strike him with full impact. He leaped to his feet with a greater excitement than Gale had shown, and began to wave an arm and shout in Mother's direction. She and Geneva had finished their exploration near the temple columns and had just climbed down into the town again.

It was a wonder Mother could make any sense at all of Warren's shouting, but she seemed to realize that something of great moment had occurred, for she began to hurry in his direction. Geneva came after her in a rush, a little like the small tail of a hurrying kite.

Warren stood on the edge of the bank and directed them toward an easier way up than he and Gale had chosen. Hanging onto a tree trunk, he reached down to take Mother's hand and pulled her up the bank. He would have left Geneva below, but she scrambled up by herself. Today, at least, she had been sensible enough not to wear high heels.

Warren found it difficult to speak in an ordinary tone, and the more excited he grew, the more guilty Gale felt.

"Look, Mom!" he cried. "I'll show you right where we found it."

He knelt and reached gently down into the hollow and set the hand into it, twitching away the handkerchief so that they could see it there in the earth in all its ancient loveliness.

There was a silence as their mother and Geneva Lambrou bent to look into the hole. Mother gave a little gasp, and Geneva cried out in sudden excitement.

"That is it! That is the very one!"

Gale and Warren stared at her as she bent closer for a better look. Gale glanced around toward the woods and saw that Nicos had heard these strange words too. He had come out from among the trees and drawn closer, the better to hear what Geneva Lambrou was saying.

11

"One Day More Won't Matter"

What happened next came about so swiftly that Gale was not sure exactly how it occurred. Geneva, still muttering to herself, had bent over the hole in the earth where the marble hand lay. She did not notice a vagrant pine branch close above her head until its twigs hooked into her wig. Unaware of what was happening so far above her scalp, she bent still lower, and the wig went sailing suddenly into the air to dangle from the branch of pine like some sort of oversized Christmas-tree ornament.

Geneva screamed as though she had been mortally wounded, and clapped a hand to her untidy, short, black hair. Her feet slipped on the loose earth, and she would have fallen into the hole if Warren had not reached out to pull her up to safer ground. Nicos must have seen the whole thing, for he threw his intended caution aside and came bounding through the trees in their direction. He halted directly in front of Geneva and pointed an accusing finger practically into her face.

"Now I know who you are!" he shouted. "Without that foolish wig upon your head, I can recognize you. I remember you very well from the time when I was a small boy, because I did not like you then either. You are Maria Roupa, and you used to work as a maid in our house. My grandfather discharged you. You did something wrong, and he said he would not have you in the house—though he never told us why."

Geneva's dark brows drew down in a furious scowl. She looked for a moment as though she might ignite into sparks and fire herself off like a rocket. Mother and Warren could do nothing but gape in astonishment, both at Geneva and at this sudden appearance of Nicos Castelis. Gale felt a little sick. Now the truth about what she had done would come into the open.

"Yes, your grandfather discharged me!" Geneva screamed at Nicos. "He is a wicked man. He has done many bad things!"

Nicos heard her. He was considerably larger than Geneva, and he put both hands upon her shoulders and shook the hysteria out of her, shook her into limp silence.

"You will not speak so of my grandfather," he said sternly. "If he discharged you, it was because you deserved it. So why do you come creeping back to Rhodes under another name and pretend that you want to take pictures of the Castelis house?"

Geneva burst into tears and began to sob and shiver in an alarming way. Between sobs she flung out more accusations.

"Thanos Castelis caused my sister to die!" she wailed. "My beloved and only sister. And he will pay for her death. I have come back to Rhodes to see that he pays a penalty for all that he did."

"You're talking rubbish," said Nicos rudely. "Grandfather never caused anyone's death. You are an idiot as well as a liar."

He pushed her away and, without a word to anyone else, slid down the bank, jumped to a wall and then into the town. Running now, he sped across quiet Camiros and up the dirt path on the other side. A few moments later Gale heard the sound of his motorbike and knew he had left for home. At least he had said nothing at all about the marble hand.

Mother took charge of Geneva in her usual gentle way. She patted her shoulders and offered dry handkerchiefs and soothed until the sobbing lessened a little. Best of all, she asked no questions.

"I think we'd better go back to the car," she said to Warren and Gale. "Our little friend here has had some sort of shock, and I think we'd better take her back to the hotel."

Warren came to life and lifted the marble hand from the hole, rewrapping it carefully in his handkerchief. "I never got to show it to Nicos," he said regretfully. "Perhaps he would know more about what it really is."

Nicos, Gale thought, had been pretty reckless and excitable. He had made up this whole plan, then thrown it to the winds when he recognized Geneva Lambrou. How did he expect Gale to keep his secret when he was so careless about it himself? For two cents she would throw away caution too and tell Warren the real truth of the matter. But there was still Grandfather Thanos to be considered, and the possible trouble Nicos had said might come upon the Castelis name. Trouble, perhaps, that had to do with the wild accusations Geneva was making.

When Warren and Mother got the little woman down the bank between them and started across the ancient stones of Camiros, Gale found herself left behind with Geneva's peanut-butter wig. It swayed gently in the wind, dangling from the branch that had snatched it from her head. Gale was tempted to leave it there. But Geneva would probably have a fit when she remembered it, so Gale plucked it from the branch and carried it gingerly in one hand as she started after the others. It felt unpleasantly limp and lifeless, though still warm from Geneva's head.

Back in the car she sat with the wig in her lap, not daring to give it to the weeping Geneva, and kept her hands away from it. Mother decided that Geneva was in no condition to drive, and she herself slid into the driver's seat. Geneva sat beside her and continued to sob softly into a wad of damp handkerchiefs. Warren was silent beside Gale in the back seat, intent only upon the treasure of the marble hand. No one seemed to wonder why Nicos had departed so suddenly, or why he had been there at all. Gale could only hope they would forget that important question.

Mostly they were quiet on the drive back to Rhodes. After a while the silence seemed to calm Geneva. Her sobs lessened, the tears ceased to flow, and she sat up a little straighter in the front seat. Mother, stopping the car to make sure of a turn, stole a sidelong look at her.

"Why," she said in surprise, "you are really a very pretty girl without that wig on your head and with that blue stuff washed away from your eyes."

Geneva cried out, remembering, and felt her short hair in desperation. "Where is it?" she cried. "Where is my lovely wig?"

Without a word, Gale shoved it toward her in the front seat, glad to be rid of its clinging tendrils.

"Why do you wear it?" Mother asked Geneva, as she took the car around the turn. "You're much more attractive without all that top-heavy weight on such a little person."

Geneva spoke in a voice surprisingly small for her. "I thought it very stylish. Also no one recognized me with this color of hair. Thanos Castelis did not know me. Nicos' mother did not recognize me in the shop. Not even Nicos knew me until he saw me without the wig. But it is not true that I do not use my own name. Roupa was my father's name. Lambrou is my married name. And I was christened Maria Geneva—so the second name is also my own."

"Would you like to tell us all about it?" Mother asked mildly.

Geneva turned her head to look at Mrs. Tyler, and Gale was able to see her expression. It was surprised and unguarded, as though she had been touched by Mother's gentle manner. Then her mouth tightened, and the soft look disappeared. She turned about in the seat and looked at Warren.

"What do you intend to do with—with that?" she asked, nodding toward the marble hand he held so carefully.

He countered with a question of his own. "What

did you mean when you saw it back there at Camiros and said, 'That is the one'?''

Geneva closed up like a clam. "I do not think that is what I said. I was merely astonished to see such a thing in that place."

"What *are* you going to do about your find?" Mother asked Warren. She was the one who seemed the least excited about the hand. Probably she did not believe it was an important find.

"I don't know yet," Warren said. "I haven't decided."

Gale spoke hastily. "If it's really old, it ought to go to the museum right away."

"Tomorrow is time enough," Warren said. "There's no rush. If it has been in the earth at Camiros for over two thousand years, one more day won't matter."

Gale threw her brother a worried look. She hoped he wasn't harboring some notion of keeping the hand. But of course he wouldn't do that. She must be patient and wait until tomorrow. Nicos would just have to be patient too. She wished she didn't feel so uneasy about this whole thing. It would be a relief to have Warren turn his find over to the authorities and be rid of it.

When they reached the hotel and Mother parked the car at the curb, Geneva did not wait to be thanked for inviting them on the trip. She almost snatched the car keys from Mother's hand and ran up the steps. They heard the clang of the elevator door as they entered the lobby, and knew that she had gone straight up to her room.

The Tylers took the stairs, and on the way Warren spoke earnestly to his mother.

"Let's not tell anybody about this yet," he said, indicating the marble hand. "If you tell Aunt Marjorie, everybody will know. I want to think about it first and examine it more carefully. For all I know, this may be some sort of joke, and I don't want to look like a fool about it."

Mother agreed that this was reasonable, and even though this was not what Nicos wanted, Gale was somehow pleased because he had not fooled Warren completely. She wondered if Nicos would have been wiser to let Warren in on the whole secret. Yet at the same time she knew that it was better for the secrecy of his plan if Warren knew nothing. She could manage to keep still about Nicos' part in this. But she doubted that Warren would agree to such a thing, even to save Grandfather Castelis from some sort of trouble. Warren always had very clear-cut notions about what was right or wrong, while Gale knew that she could be very mixed up about such things at times. Even now, when she had moved so far into this affair, she still wasn't sure which course was the right one for her to take.

On the fourth floor Gale paused outside her mother's door, still troubled and uneasy.

"What do you suppose Geneva meant by those things she said about Grandfather Thanos?" she asked.

Mother shook her head. "I don't know, but don't worry about it. Nicos humiliated her with his impulsive actions, and I suspect she was trying to get back at him in her own way. She really isn't a very grown-up person. Of course, the things she said aren't true."

"I wonder what Nicos was doing out there," Warren said unexpectedly. "Why didn't he tell me he was going to Camiros? If he stayed out of school today, he could have come with us. I wish he had waited so I could have shown him the hand."

Gale went into her own room quickly, so that her face wouldn't give her away. She still felt uncomfortable about Warren's keeping the hand in his possession. When she had combed her hair and washed so that she was ready to go downstairs for lunch, she tapped on Warren's door. He called to her to come in, and when she stepped into his room she saw that he was standing in the bright noon sunlight that poured through the balcony door. The marble piece was in his hands, and he was absorbed in studying it.

"Why do you want to keep it another day?" Gale asked.

He did not look at her. All his attention was given to the treasure in his hands. "I should think you could understand. This is something that was made by a Greek sculptor more than two thousand years ago in the great days of Camiros. Did you know that Homer mentioned the town in one of his poems? He called it 'silvery Camiros.' Now, for just a little while, I've got something that came from that very place. It's not in a museum case. It's here in my room. I can touch it and hold it and think about it."

She watched as he drew his own fingers along the curved fingers of the hand. She could not feel as Warren felt about such things, yet she could understand in a way.

"Maybe that's how Heinrich Schliemann felt when he dug that golden mask we saw in Athens out of the earth at Mycenae," she said.

Warren gave her a bright, approving smile. "That's it exactly! Schliemann wanted to keep everything he found. He hated to turn anything over to a museum while he was alive."

With a sudden gesture Warren held the treasure out to her, and she knew he hoped she would understand his feeling better if she took it into her own hands.

The marble was cool to the touch as she took it from him, and she had again the feeling that the reaching fingers pleaded with her in some way.

"It reminds me of something," Gale said. "But I can't think what. Do you suppose it's really old? A while ago you said it might be a joke."

"Not the hand," Warren said. "I think that's the real thing, but I don't know enough to be absolutely sure. What I don't understand is how you came to find it so easily."

Quickly Gale changed the subject. "Anyway, you'd better not lose it if you're going to keep it another day. It would be terrible if anything happened to it."

"What could happen?" Warren said. But before he went downstairs for lunch, he hid the hand beneath some shirts in a bureau drawer and closed the drawer carefully.

During the rest period that afternoon Gale stayed in her room to read about Rhodes in the book Nicos had brought her. She looked again at the pictures of Camiros and found they meant a great deal more than they had before. It was wonderful to think that she had walked among those very stones and seen the warm color of them as they dreamed so peacefully in the bright sun of Rhodes. A picture could do only so much. It could not give you the throbbing life of a small lizard, or the sound of birds singing, or the scent of pine trees. It could not give you the way sun-warmed stones felt beneath your hand. But all these things were now a part of her, and she could remember them whenever she liked.

Not all her memories of Camiros were pleasant, however. One thought led to another until she found herself reliving that moment when Nicos had stormed angrily out of the woods to shake a finger in Geneva's face. After that, her thoughts turned back still farther to the night when she had crouched in Grandfather Thanos' study and seen Nicos take something secretly from the locked drawer of the desk. Had the object he had taken that night been the marble hand? If so, why was it there in the first place, and what was the meaning of Nicos' action? She recalled the way he had said to her that *he* was not a thief. Had he meant that his grandfather was a thief to have in his possession this treasure from the past? Geneva Lambrou had called the old man wicked. Was it possible that he had long ago done some terrible thing—something that was now returning to haunt and trouble his grandson, to threaten Grandfather Thanos himself?

Almost at once she rejected the thought. Her own warm recollection of the old man told her this could not be true. That morning when she had first met him, she had seen sorrow in his face. Later she had seen his indignation with his grandchildren. But there had never been any mark of wickedness upon him. Surely such a thing would show in some way—if she were wise enough to read.

She did not like that thought and put it from her. The only "wicked" person she could imagine in this affair was Geneva Lambrou, and she could not help wishing Geneva did not know that Warren had the hand in his possession.

❦ ❦

12

The Black Cape
Again

After school hours that afternoon Tassoula came down the fourth-floor hall with running leaps, the way she always did when she was going to spend an hour at dancing practice. She would dress in her leotard downstairs, fling Lexine's long, black silk cape over her costume, and come rushing up to the fourth-floor practice room.

Gale heard her dash down the hallway and into the new room—which was not directly over the head of any guest. Promptly she went to the door and tapped.

"May I come in and watch?" she called.

Tassoula flung the door open in welcome. "I *am* glad to see you. I have news. Though I don't know if you should watch, because I am not very good. Perhaps today I will just do barre exercises, so that I can talk to you while I practice.

From the closet, Tassoula drew a battered cushion

for Gale to sit on. She had brought a single straight chair up to the room, and she used the back of this for her barre, holding onto it as Gale remembered Audrey's doing when she practiced dancing at home.

It was a good thing that Tassoula was so full of her own news. The fact helped Gale to stem any temptation toward giving Tassoula an account of her own morning and the strange things that had happened at Camiros. If Nicos had wanted to confide in his cousin, he would have done so.

"The first thing is news from Lexine," Tassoula began, doing *pliés* in second ballet position. Up and down and up and down, bending her knees and chattering the while. "She will be here in Rhodes sooner than we expected. Day after tomorrow, in fact— Sunday. Something very exciting is going to happen. An important American magazine is sending a photographer here to take pictures of Lexine. There is to be a story about her. Afterward she will stay in Rhodes and rest until it is time for her dancing engagement in Delphi."

Tassoula's face glowed with love and pride, and it seemed to Gale that she was paying very little attention to the position of her feet and arms.

"That is good news," Gale agreed, glad for Tassoula's happiness. "But what about the tile you were making? If Lexine is coming so soon, will it be ready in time?"

Tassoula put one foot on the back of the chair and bent her head toward her straightened knee. "That is the other thing I have to tell you. The tile is done. Nicos has promised to have it for me tomorrow. You must come to our house so that I can show it to you. Will you do that?''

"I'd like to," Gale said. Tomorrow would also be the day when Warren would take the marble hand to the museum. She wondered what the museum officials would say about it and wished she could be there. "Are you going to show the tile to your grandfather?" she asked.

Tassoula gave up her pretense at ballet exercises. "Oh, no, never! I cannot make him angry with me right when Lexine is coming for a visit. No—I will follow my plan of slipping the tile I have made in with the others and hoping that he will not notice it."

"I still think you ought to tell him," Gale said doubtfully.

But Tassoula only tossed her head. "Later I will tell Lexine the truth. She will be sympathetic. She will understand. Perhaps she will speak to Grandfather for me. Wait until you see how beautiful and gifted she is. How am I ever to live up to such a sister?"

This outburst ended on a sudden note of despair, and Tassoula pushed her exercise chair impatiently so that it slid across the floor.

"What is the use?" she went on. "I am fooling only myself. If I practice dancing until I am one hundred and eighty, I will still never be able to dance like Lexine!"

"Why does it matter so much?" Gale asked, truly puzzled.

"Haven't you ever wanted to be loved and respected and admired?" Tassoula demanded, flinging her arms dramatically wide, as if she wanted the whole world to respond to her.

"I suppose I have," Gale said. "But *I* like you awfully well, Tassoula. And I respect you too, though not because you're trying to be like your sister. I like Anastasia Casteli for the things she is right now."

Tassoula's dimple flashed, but she sobered at once. "Grandfather does not approve of me the way I am—any more than he approves of Nicos the way he is."

"What does Nicos want to be?" Gale asked.

"Not a sculptor, not an artist. Though he understands these things very well. When he was very young he became interested in the work of the Pegasus. Grandfather does not understand this, because this was never what he wanted for himself. So he thinks Nicos will be wasted as he himself was wasted. But Nicos can make something better of the Pegasus than has ever been made before. He does not want only to copy the old designs. He wants to make wonderful new pottery that all Greece, all Europe, will buy. He will do it too. He will not be defeated by Grandfather. Right now it is as if they were locked in battle. It is worse than it used to be, and there is something new about this that I do not understand."

The hand? Gale wondered. Was it the marble hand that somehow stood between Nicos and his grandfather and had brought them into a state of warfare?

It all seemed rather sad and senseless, whatever it was. Perhaps if Nicos' father had lived, he would have stood up to Thanos Castelis for the sake of his son. But Nicos' mother had not been able to do this, even though she might sympathize with her son.

"I do not wish to practice today," Tassoula said.

She wadded up Lexine's black cape and tossed it carelessly upon the carton of dancing things in the closet. "Come downstairs with me, and I will change my clothes. Then we can go for a walk and talk about Lexine."

Gale agreed, though she was beginning to resist what she felt was an exaggerated opinion of Lexine that Tassoula insisted upon building up. No one could be as wonderful as all that.

Fortunately they did not speak only of Lexine during their walk. As usual, there were so many interesting things to be seen around Rhodes that Gale kept Tassoula answering questions, and both girls enjoyed themselves after all.

Nevertheless, Gale's worried thoughts continued stirring at the back of her mind, and that night she had trouble getting to sleep. Everything that had disturbed her during the day seemed to be magnified as she tossed in bed and sought for some sort of answer. When at last she slept it was to be troubled by a very bad dream.

In her dream she saw Grandfather Thanos, not as he looked in real life, but wearing a frighteningly wicked mask as he stole down the corridor toward Warren's door. Gale knew he was going to take back the marble hand, and she knew she must rouse herself and let Warren know. That was the most frightful part of the dream—her effort to get out of bed and call to Warren. A nightmare weight seemed to press down upon her chest, and struggling against it, she finally wakened herself.

When she opened her eyes to the darkness of her room, the aftereffects of the dream stayed with her and she lay shivering. She would have liked to go into her mother's room and slip into her bed for comfort. But, she was not a baby to behave in such a foolish way. The thing had been only a dream—she knew that. In a few moments she would feel better.

But she did not. The feeling that something was terribly wrong, that she ought to get up and do something about it, persisted. In the next room she heard Warren stirring and knew that he couldn't sleep either. Perhaps if she talked to her brother for a few minutes, she would begin to throw off the dream. He wouldn't mind, since he was already awake.

She got out of bed and put on her corduroy bathrobe to help quiet her shivering with its warmth. In Warren's room she heard the opening of a drawer and suspected that he had got up to look at the marble hand again. She tapped on the door and called to him softly. A sound of the drawer closing reached her, followed by silence—the silence of someone listening. He was pretending not to hear her, pretending to be asleep. If he didn't want to see her, he had only to tell her to go back to bed, but she didn't like being ignored.

She put her hand on the knob and opened the door. At once there was a scuttling sound in Warren's room, and she saw the sudden looming of a figure against the starlit space of the balcony door. For an instant it stood there—a small figure clad from head to foot in a long, black, hooded cape. Then, as Gale watched, too astonished to move, it vanished with a rush of silken wings, and she heard it run lightly along the balcony that stretched across the front of the hotel. In the same instant the faint light from the balcony door showed her Warren sound asleep in his bed.

The dream had left her. This was real, and she knew without any doubt that she must stop that fleeing figure. In spite of the fact that it wore Lexine's cape, she did not think that it was Tassoula.

She ran to the door of Warren's room and out into the hall. At almost the same moment a door opened at the far end of the corridor, and the black-winged figure came out and raced toward the stairs. Gale had never known that she could move so swiftly. She flew down the hall more quickly than Tassoula had ever done and reached out to grasp the figure just as it reached the doorway to the stairs.

"Wait!" she cried. "I know who you are. You can't get away!"

The folds of the cloak were in her hands, and for an instant capture seemed certain. Then the slippery creature within slid out of the cape like a snake shedding its skin. The cloak went up in the air like a black cloud and settled upon Gale, engulfing her in yards of stifling silk. By the time she had fought her way out of the smother, the corridor was empty and the intruder had fled. Only Lexine's old cape remained as evidence of what had happened, a faint scent of geraniums clinging to its folds.

Pursuit would do no good now, Gale knew. If it was Geneva Lambrou, she would be shut safely in her own room, with the door locked. And she would deny any accusations Gale might make. If Mother were wakened, Gale was sure she would only tell her daughter to go back to sleep and talk about all this in the morning.

Warren's door stood open on the corridor as she had left it, and in the quiet of the hall, Gale could hear a faint snoring sound. It would take an earthquake to waken Warren, she thought wryly.

Gathering up the cape in her arms, she took it to the door of Tassoula's practice room and dropped it inside. It would have been easy enough for snoopy Geneva to have taken the cape from this room for her own purpose. But there was no way of proving to others what she had done.

When Gale was rid of the cape, she went back to Warren's room and turned on the light. If her brother woke up, fine. But he did not. He merely groaned and turned over on his side, without really waking.

With no care for silence, Gale went to the second drawer of the bureau and pulled it open. She felt beneath all the shirts and through everything else in the drawer. The marble hand was not there. She had not expected that it would be. It was undoubtedly the hand for which Geneva had been willing to risk housebreaking.

What was to be done? Gale could guess what a stir it would cause if she tried to do something about this now. Such as telling Uncle Alexandros for instance. What a long time it would take to explain about Warren's having the hand and not turning it in to the museum right away! That Geneva had been up here at all would be Gale's word against hers. In such arguments, grownups usually won. There wasn't any real proof that it had been Geneva. Not even the geranium scent was proof, since Gale hadn't seen her to identify, and the scent would fade. All Gale had was circumstantial evidence. And she did not in the least know what to do about it. Nicos was the only person to whom she could turn, and Nicos was out of reach until tomorrow morning. It would be dreadful to tell him that the hand was gone, but he must know as soon as possible.

She turned out the light and left her brother still asleep. Back in her own room the clock on her dressing table told her that it was three o'clock in the morning. She stood for a moment in the door of her balcony looking out over dark trees and roof tops toward the place where the Castelis house shone white in the starlight. Nothing stirred, nothing moved. Only the endless rush of the Aegean and the sound of the ceaseless wind came to her through the night.

Why did Geneva want the marble hand? Was it because it had great value as an antique piece? Somehow Gale did not think so. She had the strong feeling that Geneva wanted it for some dark purpose of her own—because her possession of it was a way in which she could injure the man she regarded as her enemy, Thanos Castelis.

Shivering, Gale threw off her robe and went back to bed. Once more sleep was elusive. She drowsed and waked and waited anxiously for morning to come. Then, perversely, she fell sound asleep just before it was time to get up, and she did not hear Warren when he called her for breakfast.

Later, when he'd breakfasted and returned to his room and found the marble hand missing, he came to Gale's room and shook her awake.

"Where is it?" he demanded. "What have you done with it?"

For once, it took her no time at all to become

wide-awake. She knew in a flash what he was talking about, but she had to pretend that she didn't. She hated to fool Warren still further, but she knew what a scene he would make if she mentioned Geneva. She simply had to tell Nicos first. Too much hung in a delicate balance in this affair. She did not know what Nicos was up to any more than she was sure what Geneva meant to do, but she did not want Warren to make some explosive move that might bring the whole pack of cards down around their ears like a scene from *Alice's Adventures in Wonderland*.

So she kept her secret of what had happened during the dark hours and let Warren take her into his room and show her the empty place where the marble hand had been. Then she went to work earnestly to persuade him that nothing should be said about it for a little while.

"Maybe whoever took it will put it back," she suggested.

He thought that was pretty silly, and she had to agree that it was. Nevertheless, he listened to her because he was reluctant to tell the story and admit that he might have discovered a valuable ancient treasure, only to let it slip through his hands. Postponement and time to think seemed, after all, the lesser evil.

This being Saturday, Tassoula too had slept later than usual, and Gale found her at breakfast when she went downstairs. Tassoula was still excited about the coming of her sister, who had decided to arrive on the Saturday evening plane—tonight. There had been a further phone call from Athens last night to confirm the news in her letter and tell her mother of her arrangements.

"The photographer is coming with her from Athens," Tassoula said. "He wants to take his pictures tomorrow. Lexine plans to use Lindos as a background. The acropolis there has every sort of view that is typical of Rhodes. There's a Crusader's castle, as well as a Byzantine church and the ruins of a temple to Athena. Perhaps we will go along to watch the taking of the pictures. Mother says there will be a piece in today's papers and that a number of important people will want to go to Lindos to see this. It will be very exciting."

Gale listened and tried to make the right comments, but her attention was not truly upon Tassoula's words. She had too much else to worry about. Every now and then she looked around the dining room, but Geneva Lambrou did not appear. Either she had eaten an early breakfast, or she was sleeping even later than Gale had. At least her car still stood at the curb out in front of the hotel; so she had taken no action as yet. If only she would wait a little while—whatever she might intend to do, then perhaps Nicos would have a brilliant idea that would solve everything.

At least it was lucky that Tassoula was anxious to see the tile this morning. Right after breakfast she invited Gale and Warren to come with her to her grandfather's. Warren, however, was despondent and wanted to stay close to the hotel.

Nicos waited for them in the gardens of Thanos Castelis. He had the tile with him, carefully wrapped in soft paper. The two girls sat beside him on the bench where Gale had first seen the old man, and Nicos unwrapped it and showed it to them.

Gale exclaimed in admiration. To her it looked very

attractive, with the red crab hiding among soft sea grasses, and a little blue fish darting away from his claw.

Tassoula looked at it sadly and shook her head. "I do not think it will match in any way," she said. "To know, we need to try it in place with the other tiles."

"I have arranged for this," Nicos told her. "Last night while Grandfather was out for a drive with my mother, I went to the study and took from their hiding place the rest of the tiles. They are now restored to the wooden box beneath the bed in Lexine's room. Since Lexine will be here tonight, there is no need to hide the tiles any longer. The gift must be ready for her. Grandfather is working in his study with the door closed, and if we are quiet, we can go to Lexine's room and test this tile with the others."

There was no opportunity for Gale to tell Nicos about the marble hand. She had to control her anxiety and wait for a chance to see him alone.

Aunt Vera had left for her shop, and only the servants were around as Nicos, Tassoula, and Gale went into the house and up the stairs. Behind the door of Grandfather Thanos' study there was only silence, and the three tiptoed past without speaking.

It was the first time Gale had been in Lexine's big room, and she looked about with interest. It was a room filled with airy light. From the front windows the sea was visible a few blocks away. Lexine had apparently used it for dancing practice when she was home, for there were no rugs and one side of it was free of furniture. A barre ran along a stretch of wall, and there was a big full-length mirror in which Lexine could watch herself as she worked.

Nicos knelt beside the bed and drew out the Pegasus box with the winged-horse imprint on one side.

"We can spread the tiles on the bed, if you will help me," he said.

Tassoula gestured to Gale. "Please—you will help him with the tiles? I do not wish to touch them. I might be clumsy and break another."

Nicos glanced at her over his shoulder. "You worry too much, little cousin. You are not so clumsy as you keep telling yourself. When worry makes the hands uncertain, one drops things. You were not uncertain when you painted your tile."

Nevertheless, Tassoula held back. With Gale's help, the tiles were soon set out in proper order on the bed, so that it was possible to see the beautiful table top Grandfather Thanos had designed. This was not the ordinary scene of fish and coral and seaweed. The colors had the life of Grecian light, yet they were so blended that they whispered softly of the Aegean Sea and an underwater world where delicately detailed inhabitants swam and nibbled at curious vegetation. All was perfect except for the gap where a single tile was missing.

Tassoula picked up her tile and handed it to Gale "You will place it for me, please. Perhaps you will give me luck."

Gale felt a little nervous about handling the tile herself, but she took it carefully and slipped it into the empty square. Then the three stood back to examine the whole. It was at once plain that the new tile, while it suited its place technically and did not greatly disturb the pattern of the nearby tiles, had been created in a different mood entirely. Grandfather

Thanos had painted a serious, dreamlike scene—very pure and beautiful in color and line. Tassoula's tile laughed with a humor of its own. Her small red crab did not take himself or his surroundings seriously, and he had clearly teased the nearby blue fish into a state of alarm.

Tassoula clasped her hands to her face in despair. "Oh, no! How could I have done such a thing? It is not right—it is not right at all!"

"I'm afraid that's so," Nicos agreed. "This tile of yours strikes the eye at once and cries out that it was created by a different artist."

"What am I to do?" Tassoula wailed. "The moment Grandfather looks at this, he will know and he will be furious. What am I to do?"

"Tell him," Gale said softly. "Trust him a little and tell him right away."

Tassoula stared at her for a long moment, and suddenly her eyes grew soft. "Perhaps you are right," she said. "Perhaps this is the only thing that is proper to do. Will you come with me and help me to be brave?"

Even if she had not wanted to talk to Nicos, Gale knew this would be wrong. Tassoula must do this alone.

"I really think you must see him by yourself, Tassoula," she said. "Remember how much he loves you, and don't be afraid if he seems stern on the outside." As she spoke the words, she had a feeling that the advice was sound; yet she wondered at the same instant whether she could have followed it in Tassoula's place. It was so much easier to advise another person what to do.

Her cousin nodded solemnly and seemed to brace herself. Then without another word she went out of the room.

Gale became aware that Nicos was watching her.

"You have a gift," he said gently. "You do not know it, but you have a gift. I think you speak well for your America, cousin."

"I don't know what you mean," Gale said. There was no time to puzzle over his words. "Nicos, I must talk with you by yourself. I must tell you—"

He interrupted at once. "Has Warren taken the hand to the museum?"

"No—that's what I must tell you about. Last night—"

But she could not go on because the sound of Grandfather Thanos' cane as he crossed the hall reached them. Tassoula was explaining in rush of words as she came with him to the door.

"I do not understand what you are telling me," the old man announced as they came into Lexine's room. "Show me what you mean. Show me what you have done to the gift for my eldest granddaughter."

As she watched the two, Gale forgot the problem of the hand in sympathy for Tassoula. How stern and remote the old man looked as he came to stand beside the bed! Gale could hardly blame her cousin for fearing him when he stared with such a fierce expression at the tiles that had been laid out upon the spread. She was afraid of him herself, as she had not been before.

🌿 🌿

13

The Secret of Grandfather Thanos

There was a heavy silence in Lexine's room. Gale waited anxiously as the old man studied the tiles. She was aware of Tassoula's fear, of Nicos' cold watchfulness toward his grandfather.

"What is *this*?" Grandfather Thanos asked and reached a finger unerringly toward Tassoula's tile.

Tassoula drew herself up and found her good Greek courage. Quietly she told him exactly what had happened. How she had dropped a dish upon the tile and broken it, and how she had sought to make up for what she had done by creating a new tile. She knew now that she could never match her grandfather's work, and she was dreadfully sorry.

"I helped her," Nicos said boldly. "I wanted to save her from your anger and disapproval."

There was something very like anger and disapproval in Nicos' words, but the old man paid no attention. He picked up the offending tile and carried it to one of the big windows where he could examine it in the clear morning light. Except for a quick breath of despair drawn by Tassoula, the room was silent. Gale reached out and gave her cousin's hand a comforting squeeze, and Tassoula tried to smile.

"It seems," said Grandfather Thanos, turning back to the three who waited, "that we have been hiding considerable imagination in this house. Behind this ridiculous devotion to dancing, we have been hiding a gift for color, an eye for grace of design."

Tassoula regarded her grandfather in astonishment. "But—but the tile does not fit. It does not match the pattern."

"That is true," the old man agreed. "It is also true that you should have told me at once what you had done when the accident occurred."

Nicos answered for his cousin. "If she had told you, you would never have let her try to make a new one. Her gift would still be unknown to you."

Bushy eyebrows rose in some surprise as the old man regarded Nicos. "Perhaps this also is true. Perhaps I have not been observant enough of what goes on in this house. Have you done other work of this sort, Tassoula?"

His granddaughter nodded, unable to speak.

"She has a whole portfolio of lovely paintings and drawings," Gale put in stanchly.

With careful, sensitive fingers, Grandfather Thanos set Tassoula's tile into the empty place. "We will leave it there. When Lexine comes home, we will tell her the story. Perhaps the table top will have all the more value to her because of this special tile. But now,

Tassoula, you shall show me these drawings of yours. I wish to be kept in ignorance no longer.''

A mixture of emotions flashed across Tassoula's expressive face. Gale could read her further anxiety, her desire to hide her work from her grandfather's eyes, lest he find it wanting. At the same time she clearly felt an eagerness to reveal what she had done. Eagerness won.

''I will show you, Grandfather,'' she said. ''Will you come with me, please?''

The moment they were out of the room, Nicos drew Gale toward the stairs. He said nothing until they were in the quiet garden. Then he spoke urgently.

''Tell me what has happened. Why has the hand not been taken to the museum?''

Gale explained Warren's reluctance to part with the treasure immediately. She told of all that had happened in the night, and of how there was nothing she could do without giving everything away. She had not dared raise an alarm until she talked to Nicos.

The Greek boy listened to her, his face darkening into a scowl. Yet he did not seem to be angry with her.

''You could not know this would happen,'' he said. ''Not even I could guess such a thing. Your brother should have taken the hand to the museum. But he could not know the danger and the urgency.''

''Danger?'' Gale echoed.

''To my grandfather,'' Nicos said. ''There may be serious trouble now, unless we are able to stop this Roupa woman who calls herself Geneva Lambrou. Come with me—we will return to the hotel at once.''

It was necessary to run a little in order to keep up

with Nicos' long-legged strides. Gale was out of breath by the time he dashed up the steps and into the hotel lobby, with her at his heels. At least Geneva's car still stood at the curb where Mother had left it yesterday.

Alexandros Castelis was behind the desk, and Nicos made an effort to hide his anxiety as he asked if Mrs. Lambrou was upstairs in her room.

"She is no longer here," Uncle Alexandros said and turned to wait on a guest who had come up to the desk.

Nicos and Gale stared at each other in dismay. It was hard to wait patiently until their uncle could turn back to them. When he did, he explained calmly that Mrs. Lambrou had suddenly decided to terminate her stay at the hotel. She had paid her bill early this morning and turned in the keys to the car. A taxi had taken her away. She had not even waited for breakfast. Perhaps she had gone to the airport to catch the early plane to Athens. She had not explained, and she had left no forwarding address.

Nicos thanked his uncle in a choked voice and drew Gale away from the desk. The look on Nicos' face frightened her. All of this must be even more serious than she thought.

"What am I to do?" he said despairingly.

"Perhaps we should tell Warren everything," she said. "Perhaps that's the best step now."

Since Nicos had nothing else to offer, they went upstairs and found Warren brooding in his room. He greeted them gloomily, and his expression grew no more cheerful as Nicos began by telling him about the hoax he had persuaded Gale to play yesterday at

Camiros. Gale sat on the edge of Warren's bed and twisted her fingers together unhappily. It did not make her proud of herself to hear the story as Warren was hearing it for the first time. And yet her intention had been a good one from the beginning.

Nicos, too restless to sit, lounged in the open door to the balcony as he talked, while Warren sat up very straight on the edge of a chair. Her brother did not seem so surprised as Gale might have expected. He heard Nicos through to the end in silence, with no lifting of gloom from his face and no betrayal of amazement. He did not speak until Nicos raised his hands in a helpless gesture, indicating that he was through.

"I had a pretty good idea that the marble hand was the real thing," Warren said, "but I thought something was wrong about the way it turned up so easily. I never thought of suspecting my own sister."

Gale winced and lowered her eyes.

"The blame is not your sister's. It is altogether mine," Nicos told Warren. He seemed to be taking a great deal of blame upon himself today, Gale thought, but that did not help the difficult situation.

It was Gale's turn to take up the next chapter of events, and she rushed into an account of what had happened during the night with words that came out almost as fast as Tassoula's. Warren listened and again said nothing until she was through. She concluded with an account of how she had come back to his room while he was asleep and looked through his bureau for the hand. It was then that Warren exploded.

"Why didn't you tell me?" he asked furiously.

"Why didn't you have sense enough to wake me up and tell me what had happened?"

Gale clenched her fists in her lap and answered as calmly as she could. "What would you have done if I had?"

"I would have gone straight downstairs to Geneva's door and banged on it until she opened it. I'd have made her give back the hand!"

"How?" Nicos put in. "*How* would you have made her?"

"I would have—that's all!" Warren insisted.

"She would have denied having it, and you could not have searched her room. You would have roused the hotel and exposed everything," Nicos pointed out. "There would have been a scandal in the papers, and my grandfather would have been labeled a thief. No! Your sister did the only thing possible under the circumstances."

Perhaps this was the very thing that had played into Geneva's hands, Gale thought. She would know of this need for silence and count on not having her actions revealed, even if she were caught.

A word Nicos had spoken caught her brother's attention, and he echoed it. "Thief? Why would anyone think your grandfather was a thief?"

"Because it was he who had the hand in his possession," Nicos admitted. "Perhaps I must now tell you this secret that I did not wish to tell."

"I guess you'd better," Warren said without mercy.

Nicos stood for a few moments staring out in the direction of his grandfather's house. When he began to speak the chill note was gone from his voice, and the love he felt for the old man came through to his listeners, even though he spoke in condemnation.

It had all begun—as far as Nicos' part in the affair was concerned—a year ago when Grandfather Thanos had been seriously ill. There was a time when it was feared that he would die. The old man had expected this himself. He had called his grandson to his bedside one day to give him a ring of keys and send him to the desk in his study.

"I opened a drawer that I had never seen open before," Nicos said. "In it I found the marble hand. When I brought it to my grandfather he made me put it on the bed beside him, where he could look at it as he told me the truth of something that had happened long ago."

The real beginning had been the discovery of the marble group that Gale and Warren had seen at the museum and that Grandfather Thanos had been instrumental in having excavated. When Nicos mentioned it, a sudden realization sprang into Gale's mind. The marble hand had reminded her of something more than once. Now she knew why. In the large marble piece a centaur was about to make off with a wailing child, and the child's mother reached toward him in terror and entreaty, one hand extended in the most beseeching of gestures. The other hand had been missing, broken off at the wrist. It would undoubtedly have reached out in supplication too, just as did the fingers of the lovely marble hand Nicos had hidden for Warren to find.

"When the statue was removed and taken away," Nicos went on, a note of indignation coming into his voice, "Grandfather remained for a time at the site in Camiros. He told me that he wanted to make sure that everything had been unearthed, and he himself sifted and dug through the pit for still another time after the others had left. He found the marble hand. He should have turned it in so that it could be put in its proper place when the statue was cleaned and prepared for exhibit. But he did not. He became a thief and kept the hand in his own possession. Not until he feared that he was about to die did he call me to him and tell me the truth. If he died, I was to take the hand to the museum and explain what he had done. I was, in fact, to tell the world that Thanos Castelis was a thief.''

Warren made a sound of disagreement. ''Maybe he wasn't really a thief—any more than I'm a thief because I wanted to keep the hand for one whole night. Perhaps he always meant it to be reunited with the statue.''

''He is a thief,'' said Nicos coldly, and there was no mercy, no forgiveness, in him.

Gale remembered the way he had looked that day when they had tea in Grandfather Thanos' study, and Nicos had deliberately broken the crude clay figure of Lexine. She could understand that gesture better now. Nicos was suffering because of this thing he knew about his grandfather. The gesture had been one of defiance of his Grandfather's wishes, and of grief, as well. Nicos had wanted to hurt the old man because he himself was so badly hurt.

Warren went on, speaking to Nicos. ''I still don't understand why you took the hand and hid it at Camiros so that I would find it.''

''Regardless of what Grandfather has done, I do

not want anyone to think ill of him,'' Nicos said. "He is growing old, and at any moment he might have another attack and leave us for good. So I have been seeking for some means of getting the hand to the museum before Grandfather would know what had happened.''

"It was that hand, wasn't it, that you took out of the drawer the night I was in your grandfather's study?'' Gale said.

"Of course. I had thought of many plans. Of sending it by mail. Of taking it to the museum and leaving it somewhere so that it would be quickly found. But in each case the trail would lead back to my grandfather, and I knew that if they asked him, he would tell them that he had taken it years before. So I tried to think of a better way. Your brother's interest in archaeology gave me the idea. If we could convince Warren that he had dug the hand up himself in Camiros, and if he—an American—took it to the museum, it was likely they would believe him. I chose the very place where the statue had been found originally. It was possible that the hand might have worked its way through earth loosened in a slide, until it was near the surface. There would be nothing the authorities could do except believe in your brother's discovery. As my grandfather would never be condemned for what he had done. The Castelis name would not suffer disgrace.''

"You love your grandfather very much, don't you, Nicos?'' Gale said wonderingly. "Yet you are very unkind in all your thoughts of him.''

Nicos threw her a look of astonishment, but before he could answer, Warren broke in.

"None of that matters now. There's a real thief who has the hand—Mrs. Lambrou. The big thing is to find out what she's up to. Have you any ideas about that, Nicos?"

"Perhaps," Nicos said. "That is, I think I know the reason behind her actions. After I recognized her at Camiros as a maid who had once worked in our house, I came home and talked to our cook. Fani worked for us when I was a small boy, and she remembers Maria Roupa very well. Though she has never told anyone before, Fani knows why Maria—this one you call Geneva—was discharged by my grandfather. The girl was dusting in his study one morning when he was not there. She was always curious, Fani says, and when she saw a drawer open that was usually locked, she looked inside and found the marble hand. She took it out of the drawer to see what it was, and she was standing there holding it when Grandfather walked into the room.

"There was a terrible explosion, as you might imagine. Grandfather went into a rage, and when she answered him back he discharged her. She went crying to the kitchen and told Fani the whole story. Neither of them knew what the finding of the hand meant, but Geneva must have realized that there was something wrong about it, or Grandfather would not have been so angry. Fani thought Geneva a foolish person, and she kept her own counsel in the matter, since it was Grandfather's business anyway."

"At Camiros yesterday she claimed that your grandfather caused her sister's death," Gale said. "She sounded awfully spiteful."

Nicos snorted. "I heard her. It was a stupid thing

to say, but Fani explained that to me also. When Geneva was discharged from our house, she went to her family home in Lindos and stayed there for a time. On the day when she arrived, she was in a terribly excited state. Her sister had been going out in the family caïque, and she thought it might calm Geneva to go with her. So the two girls went out of the harbor for a sail. They both knew well how to handle a boat, as those who grow up in a fishing village do. But perhaps because Geneva was so wrought up, they were not altogether sensible. When a sudden bad storm came up, as is possible on the Aegean, they were not able to get home in time and the small boat capsized. Geneva was able to cling to it until help came, but her sister was swept away. After that Geneva went about saying that Thanos Castelis had caused her sister's death. Of course, one cannot sensibly place blame in such a manner. It was the storm and what happened to the boat that caused the accident.

"Later a mutual friend told Fani about this. People thought Geneva foolish, and they paid little attention to what she was saying. Soon after, she went away from the island. Now she has returned and has some ridiculous notion of paying back my grandfather for the grudge she has against him. It is possible that she has now found a way of doing this. Though it is difficult to guess how she intends to use the hand."

Warren could never stay angry for long. He had been listening thoughtfully to Nicos' story, and now he asked another question.

"Where did you say Geneva's home is?"

"At Lindos," Nicos said. "Fani says she has a brother who still lives there."

"That's the place where Lexine is going to pose for pictures, isn't it?" Gale asked. "Tassoula told me that a number of important people might be going out there tomorrow afternoon to watch. She said we would probably be going too."

Warren and Nicos looked at each other.

"It's possible, isn't it?" Warren said. "I mean possible that Geneva has gone to Lindos to hide temporarily. She would be afraid to stay here with the hand in her possession. But I don't think she would take it to Athens, or try to leave Greece. If she means to use it against your grandfather in some way, why wouldn't she go to Lindos for the time being? Maybe she counts on our not telling right away because of what might happen."

Nicos nodded. "This is good reasoning."

"So maybe we'll go to Lindos tomorrow too," Warren said, and he grinned, all his earlier indignation gone.

"Yes," said Nicos, returning his smile a bit grimly, "we also will go to Lindos."

"What do you mean?" Gale demanded. "What are you talking about?"

"It is possible that in Lindos we will pay a social call upon the brother of Mrs. Geneva Lambrou," Nicos said.

The two boys seemed to have made a pact, though Gale did not understand exactly what they intended. Whatever it was, it did not promise well for Geneva, and Gale found herself a little anxious.

"You won't make everything worse, will you?" she asked.

Warren winked at Nicos. "Worse for Geneva, maybe."

"Oh, do be careful," Gale cried. "I don't think any of us has acted in a very smart way about this so far. Don't you think you ought to talk to your grandfather, Nicos, and tell him everything that has happened?"

Nicos thrust this suggestion aside almost violently. "I cannot talk to him! He does not listen to me."

"But Tassoula explained to him about the tiles, and it turned out to be the best thing to do," said Gale. "Even you thought this was right at the time."

"It is not the same thing," Nicos insisted. "The Greek Government is very strict today about what happens to its ancient treasures. Too much has been carelessly lost in the past. Too many things were taken from the country and are now in museums all over the world. The officials of the Rhodes museum would be shocked and disturbed by such a thing. There is nothing my grandfather can do without disgracing himself and all his family."

"Okay," Warren said. "Then everything is settled. Let's forget it until tomorrow. How about going for a swim, Nicos?"

The Greek boy thought this a good idea, and Warren lent him a pair of trunks so he needn't go home. While the nearby stone beach wasn't very comfortable underfoot, the swimming was good, and they could go in at once before it was time for lunch.

It was clear that they did not want Gale with them. Nor was she interested in tagging along. She felt thor-

oughly upset, unsettled, anxious—even a little frightened. The boys seemed to think that they had solved
everything and that Geneva would now fall right into
their hands. When they recovered the marble piece,
she supposed the original plan about Warren's "discovering" it would then be carried out. But it would
still be a hoax, Gale felt, and she did not like the
sound of it. Besides, she did not think it would be so
easy to get the hand back from Geneva as the boys
seemed to expect. She remembered the feeling she'd
had about Geneva all along—that, in spite of her ridiculous appearance and her silly ways, she was
somehow a malevolent and sinister person. Those
were perfectly sound words when it came to Geneva
Lambrou.

A conviction was growing in Gale that no matter
how angry the boys might be with her, a duty and a
responsibility lay in her hands. There had been
enough of trying to handle this affair all by themselves. It was time for an older, wiser person to take
charge. One by one Gale checked over the possibili-
ties. Her mother? No—Mother was outside all this.
She would not know what to do about it. Nor did
Aunt Marjorie seem a likely choice, even though she
was married to Nicos' uncle. Alexandros Castelis was
a stranger, whom Gale still did not know very well.
She had no idea how he might react, or whether he
could do what was wise and sensible under these circumstances. Nicos' mother might be frightened by
the whole thing and helpless to act.

None of these people would do. There was only
one logical person to whom she could go, and the

realization alarmed her. Nevertheless, she made a decision and went resolutely downstairs.

Aunt Marjorie was in the lounge with Mother, translating aloud from a Greek newspaper. They both looked excited.

"There's a lovely piece in the paper about Lexine's coming here," Mother said. "Look—here's her picture."

Gale glanced at the somewhat blurred newspaper shot of Lexine, taken at the airport in Athens.

"I hope this write-up won't draw too many people to Lindos tomorrow," Aunt Marjorie said. "She won't want the whole island there, though since this is a special occasion, some of our local officials will be coming."

Gale's attention was on other matters. She could not feel excited about Lexine at this time. She told her mother she was going for a walk and went out the lobby door and down the steps of the Hotel Hermes. Without hesitation she turned in the direction of the big white house with a garden, only two or three blocks away.

14

Gale Takes Action

By great good fortune, Grandfather Thanos was sitting once more in his garden. He greeted Gale with pleasure and invited her to sit beside him.

She did not want to risk an interruption from her cousin. What she had to say was for Grandfather Thanos' ears alone.

"Where is Tassoula?" she asked hurriedly.

"She is painting," the old man said. "I cannot think how such a thing has been going on in my house and I have not known of it."

"Tassoula is lucky to have such a talent," Gale said wistfully. "I wish there was something I could do well."

Grandfather Thanos' eyes were kind. "What you do not understand, my young friend, is that there are many different talents. There are gifts you have also. But at least everything is now out in the full light of day with Tassoula. There will be no more secrets, I hope.''

"There is still a secret,'' Gale said, bracing herself for the ordeal that faced her.

Grandfather Thanos folded his hands upon the lion's head of his cane and waited. He understood that she had come to tell him something important.

"Nicos needs your help,'' Gale said. "He needs your help badly.''

At once she sensed the stiffening that ran through the man on the bench beside her. He was reacting to Nicos' name the way Nicos did when his grandfather was mentioned. It was going to be difficult to break past the resistance and anger the old man seemed to feel increasingly toward his grandson. But she had to manage it, somehow.

In words that faltered at first, she began her story. She did not dare to look at him as she told of how she had seen Nicos take the marble hand from the drawer in his grandfather's study, of the trick Nicos had tried to play on Warren, and finally of Geneva's theft of the hand and her disappearance this morning.

Once or twice the old man started to speak before she was through, but Gale raised her voice and hurried on. She did not want to be questioned or stopped until the whole story was out, lest she be unable to continue. As she talked, she grew more frightened over what she was doing, so that it took all the determination she could manage to tell the entire story straight through. Perhaps not only Nicos and Warren would be furious with her now, but Grandfather Thanos as well.

She ended with the terrible gist of the whole matter

the thing that drove and motivated Nicos Castelis, the summing up.

"He thinks you are a thief," Gale said flatly. "But he loves you, and he wants to protect you from disgrace. He does not want anyone to know the truth about how you have kept the marble hand all these years."

There was a long silence in the garden. A little way off, birds sang among the rhododendrons. Somewhere in the distance small children shouted at their play. The ceaseless wind of Greece rustled the treetops, and the Aegean made a soft murmur as it assailed the coastline of Rhodes. But here in the garden there seemed to be a stillness that went on forever.

Gale stole a look at the old man's face and saw that a great sadness lay upon him. It reached to her very heart and made her wish that she could comfort him. At last he drew a deep breath that was a sign and spoke to her softly.

"Thank you, my young friend, for telling me these things. It was necessary for me to know. I can understand that the story could not come to me from Nicos. His feelings are too deeply involved."

"My brother tried to explain it to him," Gale said. "He told Nicos that your keeping the hand was like Warren's wanting to keep it overnight."

"Your brother has perception," Grandfather Thanos said. "Nevertheless, it is true that I have done a thing that was foolish and that may be labeled unkindly by others when it is known. I was coward enough not to want this to happen in my lifetime. Will you hear me now, if I tell you a story, my young friend from America?"

"Of course," said Gale. Affection for him, and pity as well, made a tight feeling in her throat.

His voice went on, low and a little sad, but in the quiet of the garden she could hear every word. As he spoke, she could see the ancient city of Camiros as it had seemed to Thanos Castelis on that wonderful day when the statue group had come to light after lying hidden in the earth for all those many, many years. After the others went away and left him, Thanos had searched the earth again and found the hand. It was a thing of marvelous beauty. He sat upon a low wall, holding it, as the sun set over the Aegean and evening came to Camiros. The stones about him cooled, and the moon rose very white and luminous in a dark blue sky. All these things he remembered as if they had happened yesterday.

To the young Thanos Castelis, the marble hand had seemed the most beautiful thing he had ever beheld. Partly because it was his for that single moment out of all time. His life had been filled with disappointment. To please his father, he had given up his own ambitions and had devoted himself to the Pegasus work. His dream of creating was put aside, for there was no time for the long years of work and training he would need. Still, he did not give up completely his love for the beauty the ancient peoples had created, and he continued to read and learn all he could about the great history of Greece.

The evening of that day of discovery, he sat with the marble hand in his grasp while moonlight silvered the stones of Camiros, and the hand seemed to place an enchantment upon him. When he returned to the town of Rhodes, he did not give his find to be set where it belonged as part of the statue. Instead, he planned to keep it for a few days before he turned it in to the museum. He considered that he had a right to it in a sense, for if it had not been for him, the statue might never have been found.

But the few days grew into weeks, the weeks into months, and he could not part with his treasure. The longer he kept it, the harder it became to face the explanations he must make for what he had done. So he marveled over its beauty and grace in secret until it became for him a symbol of all he had lost in life, and he could not bear to part with it at all. Nevertheless, he knew that it must go to the museum when his life came to an end. His illness last year had frightened him, and he had told the secret to Nicos. He had hoped the boy would understand, and had not dreamed of how the story would affect him. Now that he knew, he would talk to Nicos again and try to soften his attitude, at least a little.

"What about Mrs. Lambrou?" Gale asked.

"The woman with the blue paint on her face and the hairdress like a cuckoo's nest?" Grandfather Thanos shrugged eloquently. "There is nothing she can do that will disturb me. It is unlikely that she will leave the country with the hand in her possession. And I doubt that she would want it for herself."

"Perhaps she wants to make a scandal in order to hurt you," Gale suggested hesitantly.

"Do you think such a thing could hurt me now?" Grandfather Thanos asked calmly. "I am at last beyond the sting of scandal."

"It would hurt Nicos," Gale said.

"I know this," Grandfather Thanos admitted.

"Perhaps it would hurt Tassoula also, and my son and daughter-in-law. Because Lexine is famous, she could be drawn into the unpleasant publicity and all the more would be made of it, so that it would be difficult for her as well. It would be unfortunate if those who are innocent should be forced to pay a penalty for my mistakes. But I do not believe this foolish woman is dangerous. For the moment, at least, there is nothing I can do."

Gale listened in dismay. Somehow she had expected Grandfather Thanos to rouse himself and go after Geneva, perhaps to frighten her and take the hand away from her. Now it was clear that he would make no attempt in her direction at all. Already he seemed to be thinking of other matters.

"It is time for my grandson to have his own way," he mused, speaking half to himself. "Nicos' dreams are not those I would have chosen for him, but he has a right to follow them. A dream that is true and good must be carried through, no matter what the obstacles or the difficulties. The man who gives up his dream forever is less than a man—as I have been. Nicos is right. He was right when he broke the clay figure of Lexine. It has taken me a long time to see this, but I am proud of my grandson for his determination. The metal rings true, and he shall go his own way."

"I'm glad," said Gale softly.

He held out his hand to her, and she took it shyly.

"I am honored to have you as a friend," he said. "Honored and privileged. Please say nothing to Nicos of our talk for the moment. I must consider the matter and deal with it in my own way. I must be humble enough to win him back to me. This cannot be rushed into without due thought.''

Gale wanted to mention Geneva again, but she saw that Grandfather Thanos would not welcome such mention now. It was clear that he wished to be alone, and she said good-by and left him sitting on his bench, his hands still folded upon his cane as he considered all that she had revealed to him.

For the rest of the day she tried to avoid the two boys. This was not hard to do because they seemed busy with their own secret plans and were just as anxious to avoid her. Gale could only hope that Grandfather Thanos would talk to Nicos tonight and thus call a halt to any wild plans that might be in the making. For herself, while she was relieved on many scores, she could not rid herself of the feeling that Geneva was more dangerous than the old man was willing to believe, and more cunning than Nicos and Warren gave her credit for being.

Early that evening the plane from Athens arrived at the Rhodes airport with Lexine Casteli aboard. Uncle Alexandros left the assistant manager in charge of the hotel and took Aunt Marjorie and Tassoula to the airport to meet the plane. She was to return with them and stay at the new hotel for tonight and tomorrow. The photographer was arriving also, and they would make further plans for tomorrow. After the magazine pictures had been taken, Lexine would return to her old room at her grandfather's house and live there quietly until it was time to go to Delphi. Grandfather Thanos had announced that he too would visit Lindos and watch the picture-taking tomorrow. But he would not crowd the car by going with them to the airport.

Gale and Warren and their mother were waiting in the lobby when Lexine arrived. Some of the hotel guests were there too, having been alerted by news stories both here and in Athens. An electric feeling of anticipation had pervaded the Hotel Hermes. It was a little like waiting for royalty, Gale thought, and she could only hope that all would go well at Lindos tomorrow and that the boys would do nothing to cause a scandal that would spoil everything for Lexine.

The famous ballet dancer came into the lobby on the proud arm of her father, and she was clearly aglow with the delight of her homecoming. She had brought a French maid and a small white poodle on a red leash with her. There was an aura of celebrity about her, as if she were quite accustomed to the stares of strangers and rather enjoyed their attention.

She was a tall young woman who moved with utter grace. Her dark summer suit set off her lovely, dancer's figure, and everything about her was in exquisite taste. Beneath a bit of veiling her black hair was drawn smoothly back from a central part and wound into a heavy chignon at the back of her neck, a gold comb tucked into the coil. Her eyes were nearly as dark as her hair and deeply set beneath the prominence of her brows. Her cheek bones were high and her mouth large for the rest of her face. While she was arresting in her appearance, she did not seem to Gale in the least beautiful. In fact, not nearly so pretty as Tassoula. Yet Tassoula stood adoring her famous sister with worship in her eyes. And that was fine, Gale thought, so long as Tassoula did not go on wanting to be exactly like Lexine.

Gale slipped over to the place where Tassoula was

being crowded back by all the grownups around the dancer.

"Don't forget that you can paint," she whispered.

Tassoula threw her a quick look of surprise. "Beside Lexine I am nobody—nothing!"

"Of course, you're not anybody yet!" Gale told her heatedly. "How can you be somebody until you've worked as hard at your painting as your sister has at her dancing?"

Tassoula forgot Lexine to stare at Gale. "I have never thought of it in that way before."

"This time you have something to show Lexine," Gale reminded her cousin, and squeezed her arm.

Tassoula squeezed back happily. "This is true," she said. "For a moment I had forgotten."

It was not until very late that night that the hotel settled down. Because of Lexine, the young people stayed up for a nine o'clock dinner—nine or ten being the usual time for adults to dine in Greece—and everything was as gay as if it were a holiday. No shadow lay visible across the festivities, and no one but Gale seemed to give Geneva Lambrou a thought. It was evident that Nicos and Warren, having decided on a plan, had dismissed Geneva from their minds for the moment and were not a bit worried about her.

Nevertheless, long after she went to bed that night, Gale lay thinking and wondering. What had Geneva been doing today? Where was she, really? There was no guarantee that she had actually gone to Lindos, just because the boys thought that was where she was. Even if she was there, what could they do about her? What was their plan?

The next morning Gale was glad that everyone had

decided to go to church as late as possible in order to let Lexine get the rest she needed after a busy season of dancing.

Getting up late made the Sunday morning go fast. When church was over and they had lunched at the hotel, the party for Lindos got ready. They were to drive out in several cars. Gale and Warren and Mother rode with Grandfather Thanos in Aunt Vera's car. Several important citizens of Rhodes were also coming, with two officials from the museum among them. Their presence made it seem all the more important to Gale that Nicos and Warren should cause no trouble if they discovered Geneva Lambrou in Lindos. But though she tried to whisper a warning, Warren only laughed at her. He seemed perfectly confident that he and Nicos could handle anything that might occur.

That morning Lexine had taken time to go with Tassoula to her grandfather's house and had been shown the lovely gift that he had designed for her. Tassoula had saved her long story about the tile for some later occasion. It was enough that Lexine was delighted with her present.

After lunch the rest period was dispensed with because the drive to Lindos would take some time. The photographer wanted a variety of shadow effects and lighting. So off the little caravan started right after lunch.

Grandfather Thanos seemed happy to see his famous granddaughter again. On the ride to Lindos he was quiet and lost in his own thoughts. It was true that he had a special smile and handclasp for Gale, but there was no opportunity for her to discover if he had come to a conclusion about the matter they had discussed yesterday. Since he gave no sign and offered no information, she did not dare to question him.

The drive along the southeast coast of the island was very beautiful. The highway ran near sea level most of the time—through olive groves and vineyards and farms. There were high mountains in view, and sometimes one could see monasteries perched on the most difficult crags.

During the last phase of the trip they could glimpse the sea part of the time. This was a wilder, rockier coast than that on the other side of the island where they had traveled before. The Aegean hurled itself inward on swells that broke over rocky projections, leaping upward in bursts of salty spray.

The actual entrance to Lindos was surprising. The car had turned inland so that the sea was lost to sight. They were traveling at a higher level when the road entered a rock-walled pass and then came into the open high above the town that had been invisible until this moment. A curved saucer of white houses lay below them, tilted toward the harbor. Blue water lay snugly enclosed by two arms of land, one of which was a great, craggy rock that rose steeply into the air and caught Gale's eye at once. It towered above the town on the far side, looking like a great black ship riding the blue-gold air of Rhodes. Its sides were steep and its top appeared almost flat, with the ramparts of medieval castle walls crowning the forepart and running back at a level toward the rear of the rock.

Grandfather Thanos spoke for the first time in many miles. ''There is the acropolis of Lindos. This is our destination. But you cannot see what the top is really like from below.''

The road dipped steeply and came out into the town square. Aunt Vera parked the car beside others of their party, and they all got out. Lexine went to the stone wall that enclosed this space overlooking the houses of the town and breathed deeply of the wonderfully clear air. Below her, white houses ran down to the harbor, stopping just before they reached the curving crescent of beach.

Almost at once Lexine turned toward the black, rocky hill and made a little gesture of salute and recognition—as though greeting an old friend. The American photographer saw the gesture and posed her there, with the houses of Lindos below and the hill rising in the background.

In the meantime someone had crossed the square to hire donkeys for those of the party who preferred to ride the distance to the foot of the rock. Only the lower part of the hill could be traversed by the little beasts, Grandfather Thanos explained. After that, one got off and climbed. Most of the men chose to go up the hill on foot, while the women of the party were settled upon donkeys.

Lexine planned to change her costumes in a castle room up on the rock, and several boxes had to be taken up by means of the donkeys and those who could help carry them afterward. Greeks seemed to enjoy excitement, and there was great bustle and confusion and much laughing and shouting. Uncle Alexandros took command, and eventually everything was satisfactorily arranged.

Gale rode her donkey astride, and from the vantage

point of her saddle, she could overlook the little train. Grandfather Thanos was mounted on a donkey too, though his very long legs almost touched the ground on either side. There must have been no reconciliation as yet between the old man and his grandson, for there was still cold defiance evident on Nicos' part. His grandfather seemed to be studying the boy now and then, but he had made no real gesture of friendliness in his direction.

Just before they started, Gale looked about for her brother and saw that he had not mounted a donkey, but was standing back against the low wall where Lexine had been photographed. He did not look as though he meant to come with them up the rock. Gale was too far away to call to him, and she did not think he would listen to what she might say anyway.

Nicos had been the one to help his grandfather onto a donkey, and now he stood beside the bridle, a strange mingling in him of hostility and concern.

"I do not think you should climb the steps to the top, Grandfather," he said, gesturing toward the rock.

The old man smiled. "Do not relegate me to the armchair, my boy. I have climbed those steps many times in my life, and I do not fear them now."

Nicos stood back without a further word and the donkeys started off one by one stepping down from the open space of the square into the narrow streets of the town. Nicos stayed where he was, watching them go.

As she passed him, Gale bent anxiously from her saddle. "Aren't you coming to the top?"

"Later," Nicos said, and did not smile.

"Do be careful!" she whispered, and then the jogging donkey took her past him, down into the ancient cobblestoned street.

At once the closely set houses pressed in all around. They were only two stories high for the most part, but they shut out the view effectively and closed the caravan into their crooked maze. The harbor vanished from view and so did the high rock. There were only the whitewashed houses to be seen, each one facing the harbor, as was the custom in places that had their living from the sea. Once the great ship builders of Greece had lived and worked in Lindos. The houses blazed with the white light that beat upon them, with only their doors and windows dark recesses in contrast.

It was midafternoon, and the shadows had begun to slant toward the east as the sun dipped down the sky toward the opposite side of the island. Small hooves clanged on the cobbles, and there was an odor of fish and seaweed and unidentifiable food smells on the air.

Mother was riding just behind Gale, enjoying herself, but wishing aloud that this had been the Sunday that Dad could have come down from Athens and joined them. Between those who walked and those who rode there was continuous banter back and forth and little quiet. Suddenly the train moved into the open, free of narrow streets, and Gale found herself riding along a stony path that wound back and forth as it mounted toward the rock above. The blue harbor with its crescent of beach was visible again, and she could look down upon the flat, square roofs of the houses, many of them covered with dark clay to insulate them from the blazing sun.

But it was the rock that once more drew her attention. She gazed up at it and did not altogether like what she saw. From a distance it had seemed as beautiful as a ship riding waves of sea and air. But now it loomed black and harsh—almost threatening. It had a waiting look, it seemed to Gale, as though it had known so much of drama and disaster in its thousands of years that it always expected more. She had a queer feeling of anticipation as she looked up at it—a presentiment, almost, that all was not well up there. Or perhaps it was just common sense, since she was sure that Geneva Lambrou would have read the papers if she was here in Lindos. She would know about the goings-on up there today. Somehow it did not seem likely that Nicos and Warren would find Geneva in the village. It was far more likely that she, who planned revenge, would watch the happenings of the afternoon from the vantage point of the acropolis itself.

Determinedly, Gale withdrew her eyes from the heights and watched the road instead as her donkey followed its zigzag course. She did not want to think of the rock above as waiting and threatening the small human figures that mounted toward its summit.

❦ ❦

15

Drama at Lindos

One by one, the donkeys reached the place of entry, and the riders dismounted to continue on foot. Gale climbed through a stone doorway and found herself walking in the open beside Grandfather Thanos as they approached the foot of steep, rocky cliffs. Cypress trees grew here and there in this open area, standing up all about like black exclamation marks.

"Do you see the steps?" Grandfather Thanos said, pointing with his cane. "There is where we climb."

She could see the long stone staircase, built at a diagonal that ran up the outside face of the rock toward an arched doorway at the top. At the very foot of the steps an ancient Greek ship had been carved into the rock, and its outlines were still clear.

Aunt Vera came to help her father, and Mother stayed with him as well. Gale offered her shoulder for Grandfather Thanos to lean on, and they climbed very slowly, resting often so that the steps would not tax him too greatly. Lexine and her party had gone ahead, and Tassoula had followed her sister, tenderly carrying a costume box in her arms. Lexine had brought her maid to help her dress, but the little poodle had been left at the hotel.

When the steps were mounted and Gale stepped through the arched castle door just ahead of Grandfather Thanos, she saw that they were still not at the top. Instead, they went through and again into the open where a rock-strewn field and crumbling ruins slanted in a further climb toward the real heights of the rock. Gale could wait no longer. Now that the black cliffs were below, she could forget their menacing threat. She was eager to see everything that was hidden on top of this high, strange place.

When at last she stepped out into the wind at the highest eminence, she caught her breath in amazement. Grandfather Thanos had been right. From the ground one would never dream what existed here. There was so much! A tremendously wide flight of stone steps descended to a lower level, with six splendid columns marching in a row across their foot. All about were parts of the medieval structures the Knights had built, and at one end of the rock rose the dome of a ruined Byzantine church. But it was the sea cliffs that drew her most surely, for here upon their edge stood tall white columns—all that remained of Athena's temple.

Gale crossed the stony ground, circling blocks of fallen stone, and went to the wall above the edge of the cliff. Wind whipped against her as she stood looking over the wall. The cliff pitched downward at her feet, dropping straight to an indigo sea whose waves dashed endlessly against the rocks below. From some hollow, part way down the cliff, a swallow darted from its nest, startling her with its sudden flight. Across the indentation of steep sides, another cliff projected into the sea, and upon its edge a few more columns stood against a background of sea and sky, golden and lovely in the brilliant light. Gale recognized the famous view of Lindos that hung as a picture in her room at the hotel.

She turned at last to see that Grandfather Thanos had found a fallen block of stone to sit on in a shady place. Aunt Vera and Mother were still with him. Milling about were the visitors who had made the trip for this occasion, finding places for themselves, well back from where the photographer had set up his camera. A few tourists who had come to Lindos today stood apart from the rest, watching with interest and curiosity.

Lexine had disappeared into the castle itself to change into her first costume, and Tassoula, her mother, and Lexine's maid had gone with her. Waiting for the dancer to appear was a little like waiting for a curtain to go up at a play, Gale thought. She felt excited, and somewhat relieved too. All the way up, and as soon as she had reached the top, she had searched the faces of those who were attending the affair. As far as she could tell, Geneva Lambrou was not among them. Probably the queer feeling she had experienced while she was coming up on the donkey was due merely to worry about Geneva and about what the boys might do. But now all this had faded. Whatever the boys were up to, it was far removed from this high rock, and those who were up here could not know about it.

The acropolis, as she now realized, was a large expanse, and it would take a long while to explore it fully and see all that was here to be seen. For now she could only make a beginning. After she had wandered about the ruins of Athena's temple, she went to the rampart wall that overlooked the town of Lindos.

Here the white saucer full of houses tipping down to the land-encircled harbor was spread out for her to see. Around it rose rough summits of hill, shutting away the rest of the island. What was happening beneath the flat roofs of those houses? she wondered. Which house belonged to Geneva's brother?

Since there was no telling, she returned to where Grandfather Thanos was seated. Everyone was being respectful and courteous to him, and several officials came to greet him and shake his hand. Gale wondered uneasily which ones were from the museum. And would they still shake his hand if they knew what he had done? She could only hope that they would return to Rhodes without knowing that anything was wrong.

She did not sit down, but stood behind her mother, feeling that to be on her feet was to be alert and ready. She was eager to be watchful, and too restless to settle down.

A murmur ran suddenly through the small audience, and all heads turned in the same direction. Gale looked too, and her heart gave a great lurch of fright. Down the wide stone steps, running gracefully, came a figure in a long cape and enveloping hood. It ran between the columns at the foot of the steps and then made its way lightly, swiftly, toward Athena's temple.

The cape billowed in the wind, and for an instant Gale thought it was Geneva in disguise again. Then she saw that this cape was dark blue, not black, and beneath it showed the feet of a ballet dancer, encased in satin toe shoes, with broad bands of ribbon wound about the ankles. It was Lexine, of course, wearing her favorite type of cape over her costume.

As she neared the temple columns, Lexine flung the cape from her with a single gesture, and the maid hurried to snatch it from the rocks toward which it fluttered. The crowd of watchers gasped in delight. For her first photographs, Lexine had chosen the costume she would wear when she danced the role of Helen of Troy. It was a filmy white Grecian dress, and there were bands of ribbon twined about her black hair. All talk was hushed as she and the photographer worked together on several shots.

There was a magic about Lexine now that she stood before them as a dancer. The planes of her face, the big mouth and deep-set eyes, became suddenly beautiful, and there was an enchantment of grace in her every movement. She seemed to invite the Aegean wind with raised, welcoming arms, as Helen herself might have done, and there was no doubt at all that this was a face beautiful enough to launch a thousand ships.

Tassoula had come to stand beside Gale, her gaze rapt and delighted as she watched her sister. But now the longing and the envy seemed to have gone out of her. Under cover of the rustling that went on as Lexine broke her pose to consult with the photographer, Tassoula laughed softly.

"Do you know something? I have learned what I

did not know before. Always in the past I have thought of *being* a dancer—as if it were an accomplished thing. But I did not really want to dance, the way Lexine does. What I like to do better is paint, and I do not need to think so much about being a painter. That will take care of itself if I keep on doing what I am interested in doing.''

This seemed the best of good sense to Gale, and she was pleased with Tassoula.

Lexine went into a perfect arabesque, balancing on one foot, her right arm outstretched, her left leg raised straight back, making a lovely archer's bow of her body.

Gale stepped away from the others in order to look all around that part of the acropolis which she could see from where she stood. There were obstructions and hiding places everywhere. To her left, beyond a group of tourist watchers, was the crumbling wing of a building the Knights must have built. Its entire side stood open to the wind and weather, but the front was solid stone, rising to a partial dome above a window. The window was set deeply into the thick stone wall— not more than an archer's window, a mere slit in the stone. As she gazed in its direction something seemed to flutter momentarily behind the slit. But since it was a window one might look out from more easily than anyone could look in, she could not tell what was there.

Her uneasiness returned full force. Tassoula was watching Lexine's next pose, and no one was paying any attention to Gale. Quietly she slipped away from Grandfather Thanos' group and out of sight behind a broken pillar. By circling back, she found she could get out of view of that window slit. Moving softly, careful not to kick loose stones with her feet, she approached the ruined wing from behind.

At first there seemed to be no one there. But when she stepped closer and looked within, she saw exactly what she feared to see. Standing tiptoe on a block of stone to raise herself to the level of the window, stood Geneva Lambrou. She was without her wig today and wearing a bright yellow dress. She stood upon the rock in flat sandals, watching in complete concentration everything that went on out there where Lexine was posing.

Gale made no sound, and Geneva did not look around to find her there. Moving with caution, Gale took the same roundabout course back to Grandfather Thanos. If only the boys would come, she thought. She needed their help now. If they waited at Geneva's house, they would waste their time and not get up here where they were really needed.

Lexine put on her cape again and returned to the castle for her next change of costume. The watchers stirred and began to talk among themselves, moving around, while the photographer tried his camera in a new place for the next series of pictures.

During this recess Gale wandered toward the wall on the opposite side from the village, and leaned between its notches. Here she could look down upon the entrance steps far below. To her enormous relief, Nicos and Warren were coming up the flight of steps. Hurrying, she found her way to the entrance doorway and was waiting for them eagerly as they reached the top. Here they were out of sight of those who watched Lexine.

Both boys grinned at her cheerfully, and she saw that Nicos was carrying a white shoe box in his hands. He held it out and took off the lid with a flourish of triumph. In a nest of tissue paper lay the marble hand.

"You can see that we took the right steps," Warren said.

"But how did you get it? What did you do?" Gale demanded.

"It was very simple," said Nicos grandly. "We went to the house of Mrs. Lambrou's brother. We asked for Geneva, but she was not at home. So I told her brother that we had come for the marble hand that Mrs. Lambrou had in her possession and that it was dangerous for her to keep."

Nicos paused to clamber over a boulder as they made their way toward the top of the rock, and Gale prodded him to continue.

"Do go on. What did he say?"

This time Warren answered. "He told us that Geneva had left word that if anyone from the Castelis family asked for the hand, it was to be given to them. There was no trouble."

Nicos nodded his agreement. "She did not dare to keep it. She must have thought better of her act. So now we will do what I first intended. Warren will give the hand to the museum and explain how he found it at Camiros."

Gale looked at her brother in distress. "I didn't think you'd do such a thing if you knew the truth."

"Maybe I wouldn't have in the beginning," Warren said. "But Nicos has made me see how important this is to his grandfather. So how can I do anything else?"

In a few moments they would be out in the open where they could see the crowd that watched Lexine, and where Geneva might see them. Gale put a hand on Warren's arm, drawing him back.

"I have to tell you something," she said, not daring to look at Nicos. "Grandfather Thanos knows everything that has happened."

There was a sudden, tense silence. In the distance she could hear the photographer's voice and the murmur of those who had climbed the rock. Then Nicos spoke, very softly.

"*How* does he know?"

Gale made herself look at him and saw the green flash of anger in his eyes.

"He knows because I told him," she admitted. "Someone had to—so I did."

Both boys stared at her in shocked dismay. Warren recovered himself first.

"What did you do that for? Now you've spoiled everything!"

There was nothing more to be said about what she had done, and Gale made no attempt to explain further, or to apologize. She still believed in what her own conscience had told her to do.

Nicos closed his eyes and leaned against the stone wall as if he could not bear the sight of her.

"Now Nicos' grandfather will stop us from what we want to do," Warren said, shaking his head in despair. "He will never stand for the hand's being given back while he is alive."

"And if he should die, all the disgrace will come out when the hand is returned," Nicos said mournfully, not opening his eyes.

Their certainty that she was wrong shook Gale's confidence a little, but she could offer no other suggestion.

"Unless—" said Warren thoughtfully, "unless we wait for our chance and give the hand to the museum officials today while they are here at Lindos. Maybe it can be done before your grandfather knows that we have it back from Geneva. Before he can stop us. Once we've acted, he can't say a thing without giving away the truth about what he has done. Then my story will stand uncontradicted."

Nicos considered for a moment. "Perhaps he will thank us after it is done. Yes, this plan is possible. Come, we will find an opportunity to return the hand as soon as possible."

"Don't go yet!" Gale cried. "You haven't thought enough about Geneva. There's something wrong here. Why would she let you have the hand so easily? What does she mean to do next?"

Nicos shrugged and started toward the summit.

"She's up here right now," Gale persisted. "She's hiding up here, watching everything."

Nicos swung around, and the two boys looked at each other in new alarm.

"Where is she? How do you know?" Warren said.

Gale ran ahead to the place where she'd had her first view of the acropolis from the top, and the boys followed. At the summit they were not far from the wide stone steps that led down to a row of white columns. Beyond the steps on the far side of the rock was Geneva's slitted window. But now the scene had shifted. Gale saw that the photographer had set up his camera at the top of the steps, so that he stood with his back to them, focusing downward. Lexine, very beautiful against the blazing whiteness all around, wore a short black tutu, long sheer black stockings, and black ballet shoes. She was posed gracefully on one toe, her hands crossed on her breasts, a stone column tall behind her. People were in more or less the same place, but they had turned their backs upon the cliffs and were facing this way. Grandfather Thanos had turned with the others and was watching Lexine proudly.

Warren nudged his sister. "Show us where Geneva is hiding."

Gale pointed toward the ruined wing, with its dome and narrow window. "Right over there," she whispered. "She's probably looking out through that window now."

The boys could do nothing for the moment. To reach the museum officials, they would have to go down the steps where Lexine was posing, and that would not be possible without disrupting the picture-taking. To get the few good pictures that would be used in the magazine, a great many had to be taken, and the work would go on for some time.

The photographer clicked his shutter and asked for a new pose. As Lexine moved, starting up the steps, a surprising thing happened. A small figure in a summery yellow dress appeared behind her and started toward the steps in full range of the camera.

The photographer waved a hand in warning. "Hey, there! Step over to the side, please. You're right in the picture!"

Geneva Lambrou paid not the slightest attention. She came quickly on toward the steps. Several people in the crowd shouted at her in Greek, but she might have been deaf, for all the heed she paid them. She passed Lexine as if she did not see her and came running up the steps toward the camera. The photographer watched in surprise as she went by him and kept on going.

"She's seen us," Gale whispered. "She's coming up here."

Geneva was out of camera range now, and the photographer shrugged and went back to work. The three young people waited uneasily for Geneva to reach them. It was clear, Gale thought, that she was excited and pleased about something. Her black eyes had a snap to them, and without her "disguise" of wig and blue paint, she looked more human, but no less dangerous. It did not promise well that she seemed pleased.

"Come," Geneva said the moment she reached them, "we must talk."

She led the way to where sunken stone foundations and broken columns marked the remains of a building. Here they were out of sight and hearing of the crowd.

"You have the hand?" she asked, gesturing toward the shoe box.

"Your brother gave it to us," Warren said.

She nodded. "Always—from the first time I saw it when I worked in Mr. Castelis' house—I knew it must be of importance, of value. But I had to make sure. That was why I wished to make friends and to be permitted in the Castelis house. But you made everything much easier for me. I do not understand the foolishness of the American boy's pretending to find the hand at Camiros, but it helped me greatly. It was very simple to borrow the hand from him and show it to a friend who knows about such matters. I did not think you would tell, since you had no business holding it yourselves, but I knew you would come after it. Now it has been returned to you, and you will give it to Mr. Castelis, yes?''

Nicos regarded her in angry indignation. "What we do with it is not your affair."

"But of course you will return it to your grandfather!" Geneva insisted.

"The hand was found by Warren Tyler at Camiros," Nicos said, holding back his temper with difficulty. "It does not belong to my grandfather."

"What a lie!" Geneva cried. "I know very well where this hand came from. I know the very drawer of your grandfather's desk where it was hidden."

There was sudden angry silence between Nicos and Geneva. Gale watched them in alarm. She had an inkling now of the direction in which Geneva meant to go, the purpose she meant to carry out. Her opportunity for paying Grandfather Thanos back was now within reach. Of course, she had not wanted to keep the hand. Once she knew its importance, she had wanted it back in the possession of the Castelis family so that she could expose them, expose Grandfather Thanos. And no one was going to stop her.

It was Geneva who spoke first. "It does not matter, after all. I shall go to the museum people at this very moment; I shall tell them that you have the hand, tell them the whole truth of the matter."

She started past them, But Nicos moved like lightning. He circled the woman, barring her way, his intent clear. If she tried to do what she threatened, he would stop her by physical force if necessary.

"If you touch me, I will scream," Geneva said. "I will call everyone to come to my help, and it will be all the worse for you."

Gale had heard enough. There was only one thing to do. Without a backward glance, she climbed from this sunken place of ruins and raced back toward the steps. Lexine was waiting while the photographer set up his camera in a new place farther away, and Gale flew down the steps and ran to where Grandfather Thanos sat. She was aware of her mother's surprised look, but there was no time to explain. She bent toward the old man and spoke earnestly.

"Please," she said, "you must come at once. Nicos needs you. He has the marble hand. But the Lambrou woman is there—the one who worked as a maid in your house. She's going to do something terrible if you don't stop her."

Grandfather asked no questions. He rose at once and came with her up the steps, moving quickly in his need, almost with the strength of a younger man. When they reached the boys, Nicos still barred Geneva's way, and he and Warren were arguing with her heatedly. She did not see the old man until he touched her shoulder. Then she sprang about and stared at him in hatred and anger. Nicos threw Gale a look that was no less resentful and flung out his hands in despair. Now the fat was really in the fire, he seemed to be saying.

It was Warren who began to explain quickly and clearly to Grandfather Thanos just what Geneva planned to do. The old man listened attentively, paying no attention to Geneva, who hopped about like an indignant sparrow, trying to put in words of her own. No one listened to her until Warren finished. Then she burst out explosively.

"You cannot stop me! I will pay you back for all the ill you have done me, Thanos Castelis. You will be sorry for discharging me, for causing my sister's death, for—"

"Be quiet," said Grandfather Thanos sternly.

Surprisingly, Geneva was quiet. She even looked a little frightened.

"I did not cause your sister's death, as you very well know," he said. "If it pleases you to carry out this plan, you may do so. It will not matter. I suggest only that you wait until another time when you will not interrupt the work of this photographer."

"The museum people will expose you as a thief!" Geneva cried, recovering her voice. "They will—"

"They will do nothing," Grandfather Thanos said. "I have already had a long talk with them. Thanks to Gale's good sense in telling me certain things, I have done what should have been done long ago They know the entire truth. They would have gone to your brother's house this afternoon seeking to recover the marble hand."

"Here it is, Grandfather," Nicos said and opened the white box.

The old man turned his back upon Geneva and stood for a long moment looking down at lovely marble fingers that reached out to him from another age.

"Good," he said at last. "I will be happy to have you place it in the proper hands before we go home today, Nicos."

Geneva gasped. "But *you* are the thief! For all these years—"

Grandfather Thanos smiled at her, though it was not a happy smile. "Being Greeks, these men are able to understand how I have felt about the hand. They prefer to consider that it has been in my custody since I found it—as a loan from the museum. I am assured that there will be no scandal, no accusations."

Geneva Lambrou stared at him helplessly. Once she started to speak, only to fall silent. At length she turned and walked back in the direction from which she had come. She looked as defeated and limp as a toy balloon from which the air had rushed out. She had behaved badly, had meant to do a great deal of harm, yet, looking after her, Gale felt a stirring of pity for this rather foolish little woman. To live for so long with harmful intentions must be a very punishing thing in itself.

Grandfather Thanos seemed to observe Gale's reaction, for he addressed her with warm liking in his voice.

"I hope you will remain my good friend in spite of all that has happened," he said.

"Of course I will," Gale said, puzzled that he should for a moment doubt it.

The old man went on, his gaze resting upon his grandson. "I have not done well with my life. There is much to be repaired. Now I wish a few words with Nicos. Plans must be made for the future that he wishes so much."

Gale touched Warren's arm to draw him away. It seemed to her that here on this high rock where the gods of Greece had once lived would be a proper place for the talk to take place between Thanos Castelis and his grandson.

But she had not walked three steps away before the old man called her back.

"Wait—there is something I have not said. Do you remember, my young friend, that you spoke to me of wishing for some talent?"

She turned to look at him, nodding in wonder.

"You must never discount the talent of a good mind and an understanding heart," he said gently. "There are not enough like you in this world today."

She saw that Nicos was smiling at her, his seagreen eyes shining. "My grandfather is right," he said. "I tried to tell you once that you were not without talent. You will forgive me, please, for being angry—when all that you have done was right."

She could only nod again, shyly. There was nothing she could say over the sudden lump in her throat that came from an upsurge of happiness. Even Warren was regarding her with a certain air of respect.

"You're okay, Sis," he said as they walked away together. "You know, in some ways, you've got a lot more good sense than Audrey has."

This was almost like being told that she could paint or dance, and she would have liked to talk to him about it a little more. But already his interest had turned to the tumbled ruins around them. "I wonder how much excavating has been done up here," he mused. "I wonder if—"

Gale laughed out loud and left him staring at ancient stones. She wanted to get back to her mother.

She wanted to see Tassoula. There was so much to tell them both.

But one more surprise remained for the afternoon to offer. Lexine was changing costumes again, and the steps were empty. As Gale ran down them, she saw that her mother still sat on a block of stone, and she was not alone. Looking rather like a yellow butterfly that had just alighted, Geneva Lambrou perched beside her. Mother was talking to Geneva in her usual friendly, animated manner. She looked up as Gale came near.

"Mrs. Lambrou has been telling me a story and some of her thoughts about it," she said. "I think I've persuaded her that all of us harbor some pretty mistaken notions from time to time. The important thing is how quickly we recover our good sense."

Geneva nodded solemnly in rapt agreement, and Gale could only stare at her in surprise.

"She has offered to drive us to see the Valley of the Butterflies sometime next week," Mother went on calmly. "I understand it is a place we mustn't miss. No antiquities, but very beautiful."

This new, thoroughly chastened Geneva had turned a corner. She returned Gale's look with a hesitant, apologetic expression. She was clearly ashamed and wanted to be friends. You had to hand it to Mother, Gale thought. She was a whole American Peace Corps all by herself. There was someone else in this family who had an understanding heart.

"The trip sounds like fun," Gale said kindly.

But she did not stay beside Geneva now. She wandered away from the others toward the cliffs and Athena's temple. The wind from the sea was strong, and she lifted her face to its touch. With all her senses she was aware of the warm sun and the brilliant light of Rhodes, of creamy-white columns and brown cliffs, with the dark blue sea below. With still another sense deep within her, she was aware of warm happiness and satisfaction.

In some small way she had begun to know who she was and how she fitted into the pattern of things. This, she knew, was the beginning of her growing up.

AUTHOR'S NOTE

When I visited the island of Rhodes, Greece, while gathering material for this story, I was privileged one day to meet the members of a small English-study group meeting in a private home. These young people were in their teens and were working to increase their fluency in English.

They had a number of questions to ask of me as a writer. Of course, they wanted to know how I could come into a country I did not know and then go home and write about it, using the locality as a background for my stories. I have given my answer many times, but I think it is worth repeating. I go into a new place as a stranger—an American visiting a foreign country—and it is from this point of view that I write, through the eyes and feelings of my young American characters. On such a visit I am interested not only in the usual "tourist attractions," but even more in getting behind the scenes as much as possible. I try to visit homes and learn about the everyday lives of people. I talk with people in as many walks of life as possible and try to learn something of what they think and feel.

Thus, with this English class, there were questions I asked them, sometimes challenging questions of the sort that I like to ask of any young people with whom I talk. I asked what they felt was wrong or dissatisfying to them in their present-day lives. And I asked what they planned to do about the things they didn't like. In this case my questions led to a lively discussion among the young people themselves. Some felt that they wanted to break away from the pattern their parents had outlined for them. Some felt that more educational opportunities should be opened to them. Some of the girls were eager to go into professional life as lawyers or doctors. They all loved Greece and wanted to work for its progress and the good of its people. One girl spoke a bit heatedly about the indifference of some of her classmates toward anything but fun. I admitted that this is often the case in America too, but reminded her that being young is a time for fun and that there is room for the light and frivolous as well as for serious thoughts about important subjects.

The beauty of Rhodes that I've written about in the story is all there for the traveler to see, and I've enjoyed reliving it in the writing. But it was this discussion with a group of boys and girls of modern Greece that gave me the backbone for my story—a rebellion on the part of young people from old ways, yet the need for a recognition on their part and more generosity toward the good things that belong to the past.

As always on such trips, the main impression I came away with concerned the likenesses between people of other countries and ourselves. The differences are superficial. In Greece I found many friends of America.

About the Author

PHYLLIS A. WHITNEY was born of American parents in Yokohama, Japan. Today she lives in Virginia. She has always worked with books—as a librarian, bookseller, reviewer, teacher of writing, and, of course, bestselling author. She is one of America's top writers of romance and suspense. All her books have been bestsellers and major book club selections.

PHYLLIS A. WHITNEY

FOR
THE YOUNG
ADULT